All these secrets

Moira Schein

Contents

Do you want this?

So this is it? A place designed for a new breed of women. One that objectifies men, takes their pleasures and leaves. One that behaves like men had done for centuries.

Sofie stepped through the wooden double-doors into the secretive Club Elandra. It was like entering an enchanted world. Vertical gardens lined the entrance and pan flutes played on hidden speakers beneath the extravagant foliage. Even the smells were different. An artisan scent flowed through the dimly lit hallways, like midsummer rain over a rose garden. Exquisite and rare. Spending the night here was indecently expensive. Yet everything about this place whispered 'you'll be back for more'.

Looking around, Sofie understood why hundreds of women were on the waiting list, pining for their chance to experience the club's allure first hand. And these were not ordinary women. They were fabulously rich and influential. Each able to afford anything, perhaps anyone, yet they chose to satisfy their desires with the high-class Companions from Club Elandra.

Sofie wasn't a member. She would never be. As an investigative journalist, she could only dream of the luxury the club was famous for. Instead, she was here as the guest of Mrs. Gartner; one of the lucky few to hold a membership in this elite erotic society.

"Mrs. Gartner, how wonderful to see you this evening. I'll let your Companion know you're here," the receptionist chanted while reaching for the phone.

She sat behind an opulent mahogany desk like a gatekeeper to the realm of deep desires and dark fantasies.

Mrs. Gartner only acknowledged her with a brief nod before throwing a sour glance at Sofie. She resented her being here and had no problem showing it.

"Now what?" she hissed.

Startled by the hostile tone, the receptionist looked up. Her expression froze when she followed Mrs. Gartner's glare.

"Oh, you brought a guest. How... unusual. Does your Companion know?"

"No, he doesn't."

Mrs. Gartner's voice sounded clipped. She wasn't up for a conversation, not without Sofie's answer first.

"You know what to do."

"Fine." Mrs. Gardner exhaled and turned to the receptionist. "I have to... cancel... my subscription."

She forced out the words and paused in between to summon conviction. Weakly, she leaned against the counter, pressing two fingers to her mouth. She was fighting back nausea. Her screaming-orange lipstick left an ugly smear on her hand and she wiped it carelessly on her oversized fur coat, like a spoiled child destroying her Sunday best.

Usually, Mrs Gardner's status and wealth enabled her to walk through life with the assertiveness of a drill sergeant; not listening or taking orders from anyone, neither about fashion nor life choices. But tonight she wasn't in control and she hated every second. No one could blame her. She was losing a very prized possession: the ticket to her satisfaction and an invaluable status symbol in her circles.

With another pained sigh, she continued, "I need to transfer my remaining visits to this... young lady."

Sofie suppressed a smile. 'Young lady' is it? Seeing one of society's most unscrupulous harpies rake her brain for how to address her was hilarious. Why not 'Blackmailer'? Too embarrassing?

It doesn't matter. What mattered was that her plan worked. Over the last weeks, she'd shadowed Mrs. Gartner to collect evidence of her infidelity. Evidence that her husband would not take kindly to. He would have no qualms about divorcing his gold-digging wife, and their prenup would put an end to her lavish lifestyle.

As an investigative journalist, Sofie applied her tactics to drug-lords and big-time criminals. Unleashing her skills on Mrs. Gardener left the poor woman rattled to the core. She would have handed over anything, but all Sofie took was her cherished club membership. Sure, Sofie could have chosen a gentler approach, but with little time to lose, steamrolling her into complete submission was the safest option. She needed to get access to Philip, Mrs. Gartner's Companion and her next informant before it was too late. He was the club's most sought after escort and with his identity a tightly kept secret, hard to get a hold off.

"Mrs. Gartner," the receptionist replied. "You know we can't do that. We're happy to reimburse your remaining visits, but we cannot transfer them to another person. There's a waiting list."

Mrs. Gartner tapped her fingers on the counter. Her bright-red nails clicked on the surface, creating the beat to her growing frustration.

"Oh my god, just do it. I don't want to hear your can'ts and won'ts."

She wasn't used to losing, let alone dealing with hurdles along the way.

"Mrs. Gartner, please. Even if we'd transfer visits, we can't do it on such short notice." She lowered her voice to add, "You know we require certain medical information. To protect our Companions."

Mrs. Gartner waved at Sofie to hand over the blood tests and physical examination she endured earlier today. For Sofie, the humiliation of proving her health to a sex club was a small sacrifice for finally speaking to Philip. His information about another high-profile client of his, Mrs. Kerry, was crucial to bringing Sofie's case forward.

The receptionist impassively flicked through Sofie's medical papers. She wouldn't grant the request irrespective of what the test-results said. This can't be happening! Sofie was so close to her goal and a receptionist hung up on rules wasn't going to stop her. Sofie nudged Mrs. Gartner to let her speak. She leaned over the counter to read the receptionist's name tag.

"Melanie," she said, "I realize this is very irregular. But Mrs. Gartner isn't one to say 'No' to without consequences. What do you think a bad review from her and her friends will do to your career?"

Concern flicked over the receptionist's face. She hadn't considered the consequences for her job.

"Think smart here!" Sofie continued. "Let Philip decide. It's the easiest way to get the target off your back. Surely, Mrs. Gartner wouldn't argue if he said 'No'."

"That's right..." Melanie's face lit up. "It's ultimately up to him to decide."

"Exactly, so ask him to come here to make his decision."

Even if Sofie didn't get into the club tonight, finding out Philip's identity would already bring her investigation a big step forward.

Melanie peered at Mrs. Gartner before picking up the phone.

"I'm sorry Philip, there is a bit of a situation down here. Normally, I wouldn't bother you... But we need your help to resolve this."

A frightened expression whisked over Melanie's face, and Sofie almost felt sorry for having dragged an innocent bystander into this battle. But bringing down a corrupt member of parliament before she could become England's next Prime Minister and do actual harm justified some collateral damage along the way. MP Kerry had blood on her hands. As the leader of one of the world's most powerful nations, her illegal schemes and deceitful conduct could escalate into an all-out war.

"The problem? Um... Mrs. Gartner wants to transfer visits to a friend," the receptionist whispered into the receiver and the silence on the other end made her hand tremble. "Philip?"

She put down the phone after another anxious pause.

"Philip is coming," she croaked while fighting back tears.

What Illuminati society is this? How can bending a small rule cause such palpable tension? Or was Philip the problem? Was he a monster? He had to be to hold MP Kerry's interest!

Mrs. Gartner shot Sofie a dark stare.

"You are playing with fire here, girl," she growled under her breath.

Footsteps approached on the upper floor, before Sofie could take in the full meaning of Mrs. Gartner's statement. A figure stepped out of the shadow.

This must be Philip. He stepped down the granite staircase, letting the echo fill the foyer. He was a man confident with commanding attention.

With every stride, the warm light of the foyer crept up his body, revealing his imposing figure. Philip oozed authority and his tailored navy blue suit made him look expensive. He was out of Sofie's league, and his demeanour underlined how off limits he was to her. But the casually unfastened top button of his white shirt made Sofie want to trespass. She never played by the rules, and enjoyed the forbidden glimpses of his muscular chest a little too much to start with that now.

He reached the bottom of the stairs and stepped fully into the light. His classically handsome face and stylish haircut made him look like he'd just returned from a photo-shoot.

Like the others, Sofie was holding her breath while staring at the man whose skill and allure put Club Elandra on the world map. Sofie's research showed he was the club's most prized asset; their crown jewel, whose client list was as much a secret as his identity. How ridiculous. He's just a man.

"Welcome to Club Elandra," he said, smiling ever so slightly.

The deep vibrations in his voice sent little ripples of delight across Sofie's body. She caught herself wondering what running her hands across his broad shoulders would feel like.

"Mrs. Gartner, I hear you have a surprise request for me tonight."

Whatever effect he had on Sofie was nothing compared to what Mrs. Gartner must be feeling; despite — or maybe because — having sampled his wares many times before. Gone was the deceitful harpy and replaced by a doting lamb.

Sofie studied their interaction in total bewilderment. Mrs. Gartner was besotted with him and would have risked the consequences of Sofie's blackmail. She would have given up her position, her power and wealth, just to stay with this man. Who is worth that much?

But even blinded by love, Mrs. Gartner knew she could not follow her heart. Their relationship was a transaction, predictable and immutable. She realized that without money or influence, she could not afford Philip's company. Just like Sofie couldn't.

"Philip," Mrs. Gartner exhaled, her voice hitched, "I've decided to devote more time to charity. I'll be cancelling my club membership." She paused, waiting for an objection from him. She took a deep breath when she realised that none would come. "I want to transfer my remaining visits to... her." A tortured expression played around her mouth as she spat out the last word.

"I see. How very... rare."

His chocolate brown eyes fixed on Sofie, and she squirmed under his attention. He let his gaze slide over her face and down her body. It left a hot trail of stirred flesh in its wake.

"Is that what you want?"

He addressed Sofie for the first time and suddenly the lights around her glittered a little brighter; the music sounded a little sweeter, and the scents became more vivid, like a freshly cut bouquet of flowers.

"Yes."

Despite her hotly flushed cheeks, Sofie's voice held firm under his gaze. There were flecks of green in his eyes, and she wanted to lose herself in this dark pool of floating emeralds.

"Very well then. I'm willing to make an exception."

An enigmatic smile flitted across his face.

Sofie couldn't tell why this matter-of-fact statement felt so flattering. But she was painfully aware that with this man she needed to take a firm reign on her emotions. She straightened herself as Philip focused his attention back on Mrs. Gartner and her surroundings became a little duller again.

"I'll leave you with Melanie for the cessation procedure."

He politely nodded 'Goodbye' to Mrs. Gartner before glancing at Melanie. She bobbed her head in reply to his silent question. It was a well rehearsed ritual, like stamping a passport for Sofie to enter the land of passion.

Philip hooked Sofie's arm into his. He smiled at her and the world stopped for a second.

"Shall we?"

Is sex better with love?

S ofie couldn't hide her smile. She did it! She secured a night with the elusive Philip, the world's most expensive escort. And it wasn't that difficult. Preparation and patience took her halfway, so the only thing left to do was get into Philip's head and extract the information she needed. Find out why her spies mention Philip's name in the same context as Kerry's most ruthless crimes.

But all logic and reasons for her visit evaporated when Philip hooked her arm into his and led her up the granite staircase. The muscles in his forearm flex underneath the elegant, delicate fabric of the jacket, when he placed his soft manicured fingers on the back of her hand; giving reassurance for the physical contact between them. His expensive aftershave opened her senses to the warm, intoxicating scent of masculinity.

Sofie's breathing had become rapid and her heart was racing. It had little to do with the physical exhaustion of climbing to the double-height space of the penthouse wing, and everything to do with how out of her depth she felt. Her only comfort was the adrenaline pumping through her veins. It would help her stay on high alert and withstand this inexplicable gravitation towards him.

"This way," he said, pointing down a dimly lit hallway.

His quiet confidence kindled flames deep within Sofie's heart and his suggestive glances made them roar to a reckless fire before she had time to stamp them out. He swiped his keycard at the end of the floor and held the door open for her to enter his bedroom suite.

Sofie hesitated. This feels like a first date. How did he create such a special atmosphere with just a short walk? Worse even: it felt like the date was successful; like she wanted to take it to the next base, already.

"We have four visits," Sofie hedged. "Today, I only want to talk."

She needed to cut off any further advances from this skilled courtesan. It was the safest option. The necessary option, because she did not trust herself around him.

"Very well. This is your time and I am at your command, however you see fit."

He smiled and somehow this rehearsed line sounded genuine and comforting.

Sofie entered the dark room. Indirect light sources, tinged it in an amber glow and accentuated the extravagant flower arrangements and delicate tapestry walls. It created a cosy yet stimulating atmosphere.

"Can I offer you something to drink?" He pointed to a small table with a heavy glass decanter and two scotch glasses. "I catered to Mrs. Gartner's preferences. But I have other options, if you prefer something lighter. Champagne? Or a Tonic Water, perhaps?"

"Yes, tonic sounds great. Thanks."

A casual non-alcoholic drink would squash the illusion this was more than a business transaction; would stop it feeling like a date.

"Please, take a seat," he smiled, handing her the sparkly drink.

It felt icy against her skin, but did little to cool her overheated senses. She picked a spot on the large leather sofa with the shortest path to the exit. Old habits: Keep your escape route open. Instead of seating himself next to her, he took the armchair opposite, giving her space and heeding her request.

"What would you like to talk about, Mrs...." He paused. "I don't actually know your name."

There was no embarrassment in his voice. To him, this seemed an entertaining diversion from his routine; an amusement.

Good! Maybe, he lets his guard down and I get all the information I need today. Avoiding a second visit was certainly her preference, even if a small part of her would be disappointed.

"You can call me Sofie."

Having eliminated the risk of this turning into anything other than a conversation, Sofie reclined moving a plump plush cushion out of the way.

"I prefer last names," he said, crooking his head.

No way she would give him her real name. 'Sofia Black' was a well-known journalist, writing hard-hitting exposés for major newspapers around the world. Knowing who she was would not only jeopardize this investigation, it would put her life in danger. Over her career, she busted drug cartels, rogue banks and illegal corporations. A lot of people were searching for Sofia Black. People who wanted revenge. Who wanted her dead. Keeping her true identity a tightly guarded secret was paramount, so she prepared a new persona for every assignment. The one she created for this one was the name written on her medical certificates and how Mrs. Gartner knew her.

"It's Sofie Carter."

She liked to keep the first names as similar as possible; it required less acting on her part and freed up brain power for other things. Like seeing through cheap diversion.

"Is that Mrs. Carter?"

"No, I'm not married." She paused, watching an emotion rush across his face, too quick to interpret. Letting it go she asked, "What is your last name?"

"Let's keep it at 'Philip'. It makes things easier."

"Easier? Or more controllable?"

Calling him 'Philip' would lure her into a deception of intimacy, while the formality of 'Mrs. Carter' had the power of dousing any illusion of emotional attachment. Just saying her last name gave Philip the strategic tool to fine-tune the heat-level of their interaction.

"Emotions can run high at times, Miss Carter. Having the option to dial them back is important. Important for both."

"Both? So you're emotionally invested in your clients? Are you going to miss her, then? Mrs. Gartner?"

"Of course I'll miss her. She was my client for almost two years."

A sudden anger flooded Sofie. Why do women like Mrs. Gartner get to enjoy Philip's company? Take their pleasure with him. Command him to make them feel the way he made her feel right now. Just because they had the means and opportunity? It was like walling off a private beach. Keeping nature's beauty reserved for the wealthy. For now, she was tolerated in this world, experiencing it as if she was one of them. Soon though it'll be off-limits again. So why shouldn't she be opportunistic and enjoy it while it lasted?

Get a grip! You have a job to do here!

"Are all your clients like Mrs. Gartner?" she asked to keep him talking and her mind off the temptation before her.

"What do you mean?"

"In their late fifties, married, rich?"

Mrs. Kerry certainly fitted that category. MP Kerry was 56, married to a media magnate and had enough lobbyists behind her to become England's next PM. Kerry had the power to reel people in and the charisma to keep them fascinated with her. Some even say 'in love' and love creates loyalties that are tough to break. Was Philip one of her die-hard disciples? Indoctrinated and enthralled by her stop-at-nothing attitude for success? If so, he would not talk to a journalist and instead alert Kerry of Sofie's investigation. She needed to tread extremely carefully here.

"Miss Carter, all women are beautiful and age is not taking away from that. Same with having disposable income. Spending it on company is not automatically bad. And neither is infidelity. It all comes down to the individual circumstances."

Not accepting such a canned answer, Sofie probed, "You've got hundreds of women on your books. Powerful women. Are you telling me they're all just misunderstood, tortured souls?"

This was an investigation, and she needed to determine how willing he was to talk about difficult topics.

"Deep down we're all social creatures, seeking physical connection with one another; irrespective of how powerful someone might appear on the outside."

"Are all your answers going to be rehearsed company lines? I can tell your own opinion is different. So: what do you really think about the women who can afford your company?"

Philip leaned back in his armchair, studying her in silence as he let the minutes stretch. He was utterly comfortable having the aggressive accusation hang in the air between them.

This isn't working.

"I'm sorry." Sofie changed tactics. "I imagine you're not often quizzed about your other clients."

"Indeed. Never. In fact, it's an offense that warrants instant termination of the club membership." His tone was flat, letting her precarious situation sink in.

"Are you throwing me out?"

Her voice hitched, betraying how important this was to her. Did Philip pick up on it?

"No," he replied with a twinkle in his eyes. "You never did the induction, so you don't know the rules. And no point learning them now. You only have three visits left. I guess we'll be lenient."

"What if I want to extend? Become a member?"

"I don't think you will."

He stifled a chuckle; something amused him immensely.

"Because I won't be able to afford your fees?"

"Perhaps that too." His eyes swiped over her blazer. She'd made an effort tonight, but her department store outfit was a far cry from the designer clothes his usual clients wore. Uncomfortable, Sofie shifted under his gaze before his dark eyes pinned her down. "Because, Miss Carter, you strike me as the kind of person who thinks emotional attachment is needed to fully enjoy physical pleasure."

Heat flushed her cheeks. Why was she embarrassed? This was the norm, wasn't it?

"I can tell you've been in love once," he probed. "But it did not last, and you couldn't find anything that came close since."

Sofie clenched her teeth. How did he know?

She indeed had given up on seeking pleasure since Damien died. But it wasn't because of her emotions, her job made things complicated. Protecting her identity was too bothersome for the little satisfaction she gained from random hookups. And getting emotionally attached was simply too dangerous for all involved.

"Of course, you think emotions are unnecessary?" she replied, forcing herself to sound as cool and collected as Philip. "How would you know whether sex is better with or without love?"

"What are you asking me, Miss Carter?"

He enjoyed making her spell out the ridiculous question she was about to ask a Gigolo.

"Have you ever been in love, Philip?"

He did not answer. He only watched her in amusement. Was he right? Perhaps true skill could never be trumped by simply falling in love? Sofie's imagination ran wild with Philip satisfying scores of women in this very room without the messiness of emotions ever getting involved.

"I see," she said to break the silence that started to feel incriminating. "Another rule, I suppose. No personal questions?"

"Yes, Miss Carter." He paused before adding, "It's an interesting question, though. And I don't really know whether a skilled partner is better than a partner in love. It strikes me that the combination of both is the ideal. I hope to experience that one day. Because..." He held her eyes, amplifying the impact of his next statement, "I have never been in love."

Yes! This is progress. He finally gave her something. Something that actually brought the case forward: he was not in love with MP Kerry, despite her power and allure. This should make it easier to extract information. The morsel of personal information also meant that he was not as impenetrable as he appeared. She just needed to chip away at his defences and she would eventually break through to his secrets.

But when she looked at Philip, victory was written all over his face, too. Her reaction must have given him some vital insights as well. With dread, she realized that two were playing this game. He wanted something from her and somehow she accidentally confirmed that he would succeed.

Classified

Sofie's spy-game had started. She didn't discover anything new about MP Kerry yet, but at least Philip proved to be as susceptible to her interrogation skills as any other informant. But her triumph about that was short lived. Philip too gained insights. Insights about her, she probably didn't want to surrender. Especially since she couldn't figure out what he'd actually learned. He rose from his chair before she could quiz him further.

"I'm afraid our time is up, Miss Carter. We'll have to continue our conversation next time. Here, I'll walk you downstairs."

When he accompanied her to the reception, he did not hook her arm into his or touch the small of her back, like he had on the way up. The absence of these comforting gestures screamed louder to Sofie than the unsettling feeling that he knew something about her she wanted to keep secret. By the time they arrived in the lobby, he had firmly turned back into the aloof gigolo. Off-limits, yet so enticing.

What a devious circle. It was designed to create a sense of loss and trigger cravings. Like a cleverly fabricated clickbait title, it left her unsatisfied, yet pining for more.

Philip held out his hand to shake farewell.

"I'm looking forward to your next visit, Miss Carter."

His tone was even; it was a mere formality to him.

"When is my next appointment?"

A smirk twitched his lips and Sofie knew she had given away too much. Yes, she was eager to book her next visit. She needed the appointment to happen sooner rather than later. The election loomed, and she was up against the clock to finish her exposé. She realized the story wasn't the only thing on her mind when Philip gently brushed his thumb over her hand in his. She wanted to see him again. This seemingly insignificant touch made every nerve ending in Sofie's arm explode. And it wasn't by accident; he knew exactly what he was doing.

"Melanie will make the arrangements with you. Goodbye for now, Miss Carter."

He nodded towards the receptionist. It was another secret communication between them; another information exchange that Sofie was not privy to or supposed to notice.

"The earliest appointment Philip has available is in three weeks."

It was an eternity for a fast-moving investigation like hers, and Sofie wasn't sure whether the nod had a positive or negative influence on the timing. With a sigh, she agreed. At least it gave her enough time to collect background information on Philip. Knowing his identity should make it pretty easy to follow him after work and find out what this enigmatic gigolo was up-to in his private life.

At least that's what Sofie thought, but two weeks later, she wasn't any closer to unearthing the man behind the myth. She tapped the steering wheel of her car in frustration.

She had been surveying Elandra, either in person or through her hidden cameras, and during all that time Philip has not left the compound even once. He stayed away from prying eyes, behind the barbed wire fencing and safely out of the reach of blackmailers like her. Smart choice, given the power and influence of his clients.

The only people leaving through the single patrolled gate were the catering and cleaning crew. There was no point in following them since they were new people every day. The agency sending them did not know who would be assigned on any given day. According to them, Elandra would hand-pick the crew in the morning amongst the agency's most experienced staff. So sneaking herself in as an extra crew member wouldn't work either.

It was well after midnight again. A slight drizzle created a dull drub on the roof of the car that sent Sofie into a brooding gloom. Another day wasted. Displeased, Sofie watched the receptionist hurry to her white sedan. She was the only permanent staff member living outside the high security compound and it was the end of her shift.

Maybe Sofie needed to broaden her focus? Maybe the harmless Melanie had confidential information about Philip that would prove useful? Sofie started her engine. Better than sitting around here.

Sofie knew she was onto something as soon as Melanie took the offramp to the commercial dock area instead of heading home to bed, as Sofie had expected her to do. The white sedan crept along the gravel road next to towering containerships and pitch black warehouses. Why would anyone head to the docks at night? It was dangerous, especially for a woman. Maybe the receptionist wasn't so harmless, after all?

Melanie parked her car next to a dilapidated wooden storage building. The massive rolling barn doors were slightly open, letting a brutal white glare of fluorescent light flood on the pavement. Even through the closed car doors, Sofie heard the cheer of a large crowd inside the building. What was this place? Only one way to find out. Sofie closed her car door when a bone-curling cry froze her in place.

It wasn't human, that much was clear. But she couldn't tell what type of animal it belonged to, only that it was screaming in pain.

Sofie's heart raced. This was an illegal animal fighting arena; probably dogs or roosters, judging by the size of the ring. The metallic stench of blood cut through the fumes of cheap alcohol and the pungent sweat oozing from the low-lives who feasted on the pain of helpless animals.

"The winner is... Frankenclaw," exclaimed a man on a podium with faked excitement.

Melanie lingered on the railing close to the man, but she faced away from the arena and red smeared sawdust below.

"Alright folks, we'll be back in 5. Get your bets in, it's Terminator versus...", the man turned to Melanie and whispered something in her ear that made her smile, "Beakzilla. Should be a good fight."

Sofie was pushing her way through the dispersing crowd when a middle-aged woman with a bulging red nose grabbed her arm.

"Hey." She planted herself in front of Sofie, breaking her line of sight to Melanie. "You're new, yeah? Wanna make money? I give you tips!"

"No, thanks. I know my way around."

Sofie turned away from the revolting smell of booze and stale cigarettes. The woman tumbled forward, reaching with one hand for Sofie's shoulder to support her weight, while the other felt up her pockets.

"Ah, you're rich, hon! I'll make you richer. But you need to be nicer to me."

With one effortless move, Sofie grabbed the woman's hand and bent her fingers backwards.

"You see this?" Sofie said evenly, while the woman winced in pain. "This is the nicest I'll be. So stay away from me."

Sofie didn't lose her temper easily, but she was angry. Not because of the woman but because of the hard choice she had to make: report the illegal animal fighting club and give up on Melanie as her informant, or turn a blind eye and secure someone on the inside, who would report back on Philip.

With a heavy heart, Sofie approached Melanie.

"Oh shit," the receptionist cursed as she recognized Sofie. "What are you doing here?"

"I followed you."

"Why?"

"Why do you think?"

"You wanna get me fired! Your stunt with Mrs. Gartner almost did it, and now this..."

"Do you want to keep your job?"

"No." Melanie's answer came without hesitation. What was she playing at?

"No? Good, then you won't mind the email going out at 7am, telling Elandra about what you are up to here." Sofie turned to leave. She needed to dial up the heat.

"Wait..."

"Oh, so you don't want Elandra to know about your little side hustle? You're with the organizer. Right? Is he your boyfriend?"

"Husband..." Melanie volunteered, sounding less sure of herself. "I'm trying to get out. Henry said it was the fastest way to get money for the passports.

"What do you mean 'out'?"

"Elandra is not just an employer. They are... I don't know.... They have power. You're not just simply quitting a job with them and walk away." Fear resonated in her voice.

"Was that what happened when you called Philip to transfer Mrs. Gartner's visits? Did he threaten you?"

"No. Philip wouldn't... he's not like them."

"Because he's staff, like you?"

"No, that's not it. He is the Primo. He absolutely is one of them, but he behaves... differently."

"How so?"

Melanie shook her head as she nervously chewed her lip.

"I've said too much already."

"Melanie, you've given me enough to cause problems for you but not enough for me to protect you."

The receptionist looked tortured and confused.

"How can I trust you?"

"This isn't about trust. It's about benefits. If you become my informant at Elandra, I'll want to keep you there and won't send my email. I'm giving you a chance to carry on as before. Do you really want to risk that?"

Malanie's eyes filled with tears as she shook her head in defeat.

"Then tell me how Philip is 'different'."

"Ok. I'll. Tell. You," she sobbed before getting a grip on herself. "None of the companions can communicate with the outside world. They don't have a phone, internet or TV. The only thing to keep them informed is newspapers. So Philip gives me ads to put in the 'classified' section of The Daily Guardian. I think he communicates with someone through that."

Sofie stared at Melanie. Elandra sounded like an evil cult, isolating its members and controlling their access to information. Melanie was right to fear them.

"Do you have one of Philip's ads?"

"No. I burn them as soon as I post the ads. But I remember the last one, because it was so odd. It was about a 20-year-old female who's into politics and was looking for a 80-year-old man to go on hunting trips with. In Karlingford or Durbigsher. I didn't know you could hunt there."

"You can't."

Sofie smiled. 'Karlingford or Durbigsher' wasn't referring to a place. It was 'Carl Durbing', the name of a hitman. And not just any hitman, it was the one MP Kerry used to kill her opponent. Sofie uncovered his name but little more about the circumstances. Philip communicated his knowledge to someone on the outside.

"What does it mean, then?"

"How would I know?" Sofie lied. Melanie didn't need to know any of this. "Quite an age discrepancy too."

"Yes, another odd thing with that one. He has never included an age before." The receptionist huffed, "I had to always argue with the newspaper about that because it's a mandatory field."

Odd indeed. Maybe the numbers weren't ages at all, maybe they were dates? Twenty and eighty could mean 20.08.? How was this linked to the murder? It was two months after the murder.

"When was the last time he posted an ad?"

"He usually gives me a new ad to post every Monday, but he hasn't given me one in over two weeks."

Why? Did someone discover their communications? Or did he tell the informant everything he knew? The explanation for why he stopped would be in the answer from his contact; one of the newer ads in the newspaper. Sofie just needed to find it.

"Thanks, you've helped a lot. I won't tell Elandra about any of this." Sofie placed a hand on Melanie's shoulder. "Melanie, you know this is cruel and illegal. You need to do the right thing and shut this down. You and your husband will have to find other ways to earn money."

"OK." Her voice sounded strangely relieved, like she had been waiting for someone to force them to shut down.

As soon as Sofie was back in her car, she pulled out her phone to search the classified ads section for the keywords "hunting" and "politics" over the past three weeks. Four ads popped up on her screen:

ID #22456 Seeking: 30 to 50 conservative, political, single or divorced female who loves hunting and crocheting. I (40) like travel and baking.

ID #22456 Female, politics-buff (24) looking for male (50) to go hunting in Karlingford or Durbigsher.

That's Philip's ad! Melanie remembered the ages wrong: Twenty-four and fifty would be 24.05. That makes more sense. It was fourteen days before the murder. Philip was likely telling someone when Kerry contracted Durbing to arrange the hit. Sofie scrolled through the next one. She still needed to find the answer from Philip's contact.

ID #22544 Female (30) into politics and hiking. I'm adventurous and loving. Hunting for love or marriage.

ID #23045 Male hunting enthusiast. No luck in Durbigsher. Ready to move on with new interests. Looking for s/o to put my feet up in front of a fire.

That must be it. Philip's contact told him that he or she could not reach Carl Durbing and that they didn't want to pursue this investigation any longer. Philip stopped his ads because his contact wanted out. Was the last sentence telling him that they got cold feet? It wouldn't be surprising, MP Kerry was a powerful opponent, and going against her wasn't something a private investigator would consider, especially when there was no key witness.

Sofie let out a laugh. That's what he learned about her. He somehow deduced that she had come for the information rather than his services. Good. That way, next week's meeting would be less of a struggle for her self-control and she would finally find out what motivated Kerry to commit murder when she had other options at her disposal.

Indecent proposal

S ofie sat opposite Philip in Elandra's elegant restaurant. They met for lunch and instead of Philip's bedroom suite, he had led her to the sandstone veranda overlooking the rolling English countryside. Sofie breathed a sigh of relief. In this public setting, she could focus on getting the information she needed without getting distracted by their chemistry.

"Before I left last time, you had a strange look on your face," she opened, hoping to get straight to the point by confirming his hunch about her. Then they could discuss how to exchange information, negotiate payments, and she could get on with her story. When it came down to it, all informants were basically the same: give them carrots or sticks and they will talk.

"What look?"

"Like I can give you something you need."

"Hmm." A curt nod acknowledged her observational skills; he had not expected her to interpret his expression so clearly. "Maybe you can, maybe you can't. This isn't about me. It's about you. What do you want?"

He sandbagged her. He knew she wanted information, no need to spell that out. Instead he asked about her motives. Why? They never mattered to anyone in the past. All people cared about was what's in it for them. So why did it matter to him? Did he want to actually sell dirt on MP Kerry? Or was he hired to sound out Kerry's opponents? If so, he wanted to find out what Sofie already knew about MP Kerry and report the details back. She needed to be careful, needed to first find out where his allegiances lied.

"No. You cannot answer a question with a question, Philip."

A sly smile crept into his face, bringing back the confident gigolo.

"Well, Miss Carter, it would seem that I can." The midday sun sparked in his drink and reflected mischievously in his eyes. "And I would argue that my question is more interesting than yours. Because what I want is quite obvious. I told you so last time: I've never been in love."

What? He tried to bait her. How insufferably cocky. He seemed to think that saying he'd never been in love was like waving a red flag in front of a bull. This might work on women with the psychological profile of his clients, used to winning every challenge, but it didn't work on her. Philip had already decided this was a challenge no one would win, and it merely amused him seeing them try.

That was fine by her. Her goal wasn't to get into his heart. She wanted to get into his head. Fortifying his defences at the wrong spot would only make her job easier.

"Ok. You want to know why I'm here?" She looked down at her hands. "When Mrs. Gartner told you she wanted to quit the Club, she mentioned her charity work. That's how we met. I helped her understand that the pleasures here are meaningless distractions to what really matters in life. But she has a hard time letting go and I tease her about it. So we made a bet: If I give into the delights here, I don't get to ridicule her anymore."

"Really? You're a charity worker?"

"Yes. I help the homeless."

It was close enough to the truth. In fact, stopping MP Kerry probably did more for the homeless than the soup kitchen and shelters combined. It would stop a further deterioration of the already meager social support net and prevent more people from slipping into poverty. It also gave her the perfect alibi for why she met with unsavoury characters, or ducked through dangerous alleyways at night.

"And Mrs Gartner helps too? I didn't think she's the type." He almost laughed at the absurdity. "It's tough work. Good that she has you for moral support. Though I assume it's not mutual. Who supports you when you need it?"

"Are you asking me if I have a partner?"

He's good! He planted the idea, once more, that he was actually interested in her. That this might turn into love.

"Do you?"

"No. My work fulfils me."

She, too, had rehearsed lines.

"Well then," he smiled, "that brings me back to my original question: What do you want? Why did you really agree to come here, Miss Carter?"

Did he just outmanoeuvre her? Well played. But there were many ways to parry a strike, even a clever one.

"Curiosity, I suppose," she offered, gearing up for a strike of her own. "I didn't really want to take Mrs. Gartner up on her offer. I thought the club would never transfer the visits. Not to someone like me. So, coming here

and playing along seemed the easiest way to get Mrs. Gartner off my back."
She exhaled slowly. "But when I saw you... And you asked me if I wanted
this..." she looked at his lips, "all I could think was 'Yes'."

She shook her head, pretending to be embarrassed.

"Oh my god. I'm never spontaneous like this. But I'm sure you see this all
the time." She looked up at him from under her lashes. "I know you said
you don't want to talk about the others, but it would make me feel... less
silly." She made her voice tremble slightly. "I need to know that others trust
you like this too."

She only needed a small opening. Once he started talking about his other
clients, it would be easy to steer the conversation to MP Kerry.

Once he started talking about his other clients, it would be easy to steer the
conversation to MP Kerry.

"Oh, you are skilled," he smiled, savouring her shock of being called out.
"I even want to believe you. And when you looked at me like that..." He
bit his lower lip and tapped two fingers against his heart. "I almost had
butterflies."

Darn! It had been a while since anyone saw through her ruses. He was
clearly too observant to be played. This was going nowhere! She should
just get up and leave. Yet something kept her in place. Some magnetic force
locked her inside his presence.

"But," he disrupted her brooding, "the part about you wanting to trust me?
It's the first true thing you've said to me."

He took a sip from his tonic, evaluating her.

"You wanted to achieve something here today, Miss Carter. But it isn't going as planned. I can tell that you don't think you'll get there anymore. Yet you are staying. What keeps you here, Miss Carter?"

Not you, you self-centred prick. It's because I don't give up! What I fight for is worth it. And I might still come up with a solution. Just you see.

She took a deep breath. As her anger subsided, she had to admit that calling her charade was a neat trick. This man was skilled at reading people; at observing and making the right deductions. It probably made him the incredible lover he was famed for.

But they had come to a crossroad. Neither of them would crack accidentally and spill the true reason for their interest. Whoever wanted this more had to show their hand deliberately and forge an inroad for the other to follow. 'Be honest' or 'Give up'. Neither looked appealing to Sofie.

"I tell you what," Philip said, playing with the condensation on his glass. "I'll describe to you how these visits go."

Fine. She needed to regroup and come up with a new strategy. Him gloating about his skills gave her the time to think. Hopefully, it wouldn't be too explicit. The thought of listening to how he seduced other women was strangely hard to stomach.

"The physical act of intimacy," he started in a voice as smooth as honey, "is the smallest part of the visit. It's not unusual for me to have a conversation with the women for two of the three hours we're together. A subtle dance, if you will, to learn how to read her. Helping our minds connect before our bodies do. Rather similar to what we're doing now".

Heat rose in Sofie's cheeks. The next hour could be quite different if she gave into her desires.

"Sometimes these conversations bring up memories," he continued, focusing her thoughts away from the lust spreading in her body. "You see, I'm a collector. I collect these memories like others might collect butterflies. And just like the wings of butterflies, the specimens in my collection are very sensitive; easily disturbed by the harsh light of day. So I guard them. I don't show them to people. But..." He lightly tapped his finger on the table. Was he nervous? "I'm willing to show some of my butterflies to a fellow collector who appreciates their value." He paused to gather her full attention. "Would you be such a collector?"

He did it! He played his hand first. He wanted to share the secrets about his clients with Sofie. Wanted to make her his new contact.

"Yes," she replied, careful to not let her smug glee seep through.

"I thought so," he exhaled, undermining the confidence in his statement. "As a fellow collector, Miss Carter, you'll appreciate how fragile my specimens are. One wrong move, one malicious touch, one selfish action could cause real damage."

That's why he asked about her motives. He wasn't trying to sell her out or maximize his gain. He simply wanted to make sure that neither was she.

"My reason for accessing your collection is neither malicious nor selfish. But Philip..." She didn't want to disclose too much, but neither mislead him. "If I do my job right, the specimen you show me will get damaged."

It was Sofie's way of rewarding his trust, giving him something in return. It wasn't much, but it was all she could offer at this stage. And it was still a risk. Either he wanted to damage Kerry and their conversation could continue, or he would shut this down right now.

"I see," he replied with a nod that acknowledged her honesty. "If you have such good use for my collection, you'll understand that there will be a price for accessing it."

"Of course. What do you have in mind?"

Sofie was back on familiar ground: working out deals, negotiating terms, that's what she loved doing. Every story she worked on had winners and losers. Typically, the ones who talked early came out with the best deal: money, immunity, protection. It was her job to broker between opposing sides, each protecting something; be that their interest or the law.

"The price, Miss Carter, is something equally well guarded."

An enigmatic smile crossed his face as he let his gaze glide up her long legs, over the curve of her hips, before burning the weight of his meaning into her mind.

The breath went out of Sofie's lungs. She had indecent proposals before. Every single one of them was laughable or downright demeaning. With this one, though, she wasn't laughing or disgusted. This one actually felt dangerous. Dangerous because she wanted to pay the price; wanted to pay upfront without even checking the goods. But her journalistic training kicked in and the questions tumbled from her lips, before her emotions betrayed her.

"Why? You have a new woman every night. Why me?"

"You are..." He paused. His eyes dropped to her mouth, lingering, before he inhaled sharply, as if to drag his mind away from something. "It's a test, Miss Carter. A test to see how much my butterflies are worth to you. How wisely you'll use them."

Holding the secrets of powerful women wasn't a commodity to be auctioned off to the highest bidder. There would be consequences to him and the women involved. He wanted her to consider these consequences by weighing them against a personal price. Was this his conscience speaking? Or was he just playing with her?

"But Philip, with this arrangement, I'm not the only one paying a price. You'd pay too."

He chuckled.

"In case you don't remember: I sleep with women for a living," he said before a dark expression took over his face." One more doesn't make a difference to me. For me, it would be utterly forgettable."

The ice in his voice made her shudder. He implied that while it meant nothing to him, it wouldn't be forgettable for her. That she had to give up the sovereignty of her body to get a deal. That her actions would weigh on her conscience long after the physical act was over. But there also was a fire in his eyes that suggested a different interpretation. It would be unforgettable because she'd gain an experience; an experience Club Elandra would pride itself on.

Was her story worth the price? Was she willing to play against this master-manipulator, and confident enough to come up on top in such a dangerous game?

Creature of luxury

Sofie's cheeks were flushed and she had to collect her thoughts. Philip wanted to share his secrets but only as part of an unsavoury deal. Not out of passion or as a power play, it was a test. A test to determine if she could be trusted with the explosive information he was going to provide.

"That's a steep price. How do I know you actually have anything worth that much?" Sofie asked.

"I love your confidence." He almost laughed, shaking his head. "Let me assure you that the information I have is worth far more than whatever value you place on a night with you."

Seeing her anger rise, he leaned closer to add, "Not because you are not beautiful or unique... you absolutely are," he paused to observe how his calculated compliment affected her. "But because you are only one person. Getting the information into the wrong hands, now that would have consequences for a lot more people."

"Including you?"

Gone was her anger, replaced by genuine concern. She knew that Kerry's secrets were deadly. And Philip was the first in the firing line.

"Likely," he said with a dangerous smile.

He likes playing with fire.

"Ok, let's assume you have valuable secrets, in general. How do I know you've got the one I'm interested in?"

"Did you know," he replied as if to divert the topic, "that the Monach Butterfly is considered the queen of the butterflies? Do you know where the name comes from?"

"Um, because it's the largest butterfly?" Sofie knew nothing about butter-flies but was playing along to humor him.

"Sure, it's big and beautiful, but that's not where the name comes from. It's because it has a very unique skill... It can cheat death."

Where was this conversation going?

"You see..." His words were dripping with subcontext, "most butterflies only live three weeks. But if a Monarch butterfly is born just before winter, it becomes skilful and determined to survive for eight months. During that time it migrates; conquering and ruling above the laws of physics."

Conquering and ruling? Was he talking about MP Kerry?

Kerry certainly saw herself above the law and god knows what she was planning to do as Prime Minister. But even if he was talking about her, being driven and skilful wasn't a secret. Some of her supporters hailed them as the qualities that set her apart from the other politicians. The real question was: did Philip have dirt on her?

Sensing her doubt he continued, "the secret to this uncanny longevity lies in its genes. Scientists have created a machine that can read these secrets. It's not much larger than a USB stick."

Sofie swallowed.

A USB stick to read secrets?

This wasn't an article from a New Scientist magazine! He was talking about a YubiKey, a device that looks just like an USB stick but functions as a digital key to protect online information. Was he telling her that he had Kerry's YubiKey?

"Is that valuable enough for you?" He smiled, pleased with how Sofie caught his meaning.

Sofie's heart raced. This was better than she could have hoped for. The key was the central part of Kerry's two-factor authentication system. By giving it to her, Philip was essentially serving her all of Kerry's shady deals on a silver platter.

Philip leaned back in his chair. He looked relaxed. Calm. Oblivious.

He doesn't know! He thinks he only gives away the key but not the actual access.

Sofie steeled her features. He didn't need to know that the key was the only thing she still needed to gain access. She already had the second part of the two-factor system: the password.

It was 'Kerry4PM'. Kerry for Prime Minister. Utterly predictable, yet it took Sofie's spies nearly two months to find it out. Kerry rarely had to type it in. It was only needed to authorize new devices and only worked in conjunction with the YubiKey; something you know, and something you have.

When her spies got the password for her, Sofie never actually expected to use it. Because getting her hands also on the key was considered impossible. The MP wore it around her neck and had a proximity alarm on it. Stealing, "borrowing" or copying it was out of the question, essentially making the password useless to Sofie. 'Something you know' is worthless without 'Something you have'.

Just like Philip probably thought the key would be worthless to Sofie without the password. Well, he was wrong! And soon she would have an all-area access pass to Kerry's secrets.

Hang on! Sofie's alarm bells started ringing. This was too good to be true. Why would Kerry give the key to Philip? A Gigolo, out of all people? He certainly wasn't the most trustworthy person in her network.

Dammit! This left only one conclusion: Philip was lying! He was just playing with her.

"'Valuable'? More like 'unbelievable'! Why would you have the USB stick?"

"What USB stick?" he asked with mock surprise, "The one to read butterfly genomes? Why would I have such a thing? I'm not a scientist."

Sofie took a quick look around the empty restaurant, before lowering her voice and biting out, "the YubiKey!"

"Ah," he smiled as if she had just uttered the magical pass phrase to the thieves' den.

"It's the backup," he replied mimicking Sofie's hushed voice. "For emergency access. In case the other one's lost."

"But why would she give that to you? Why not her husband? Or her staff? Or put it in a safe?"

Philip reclined and let his eyes glide over the green hillside beyond the veranda.

"Did you know," he said in a similar tone to his first story," that the Owl Butterfly has a very special marking on its wings? Do you know what it looks like?"

"No. I. don't."

"C'mon, take a guess."

"An owl?" Sofie sighed.

"Almost," he smiled "It looks like the eye of an owl. One eye, to be precise. It needs to find a partner so that they together can pretend to be an owl. Two eyes looking at their enemies."

Sofie stared at him blankly. The frustration of having to play along with his ridiculous games was mixing with the fury of not even getting the meaning this time. She had no clue how to decipher his riddle. Why would MP Kerry need a second butterfly? For protection? Unless...

MP Kerry and Club Elandra were each powerful. But together, they were impenetrable. No one would dare to make an enemy of both at the same time.

Sofie grinned. Except her. Yes, she was that daring, not afraid to jump into danger with both feet. Not beating around the bush. It wasn't her style. And that's precisely why Philip's puzzles were getting on her nerves. Either he was willing to talk or not. No need to make a game of it.

"Why do you speak in riddles?"

"I immensely enjoy playing with you, Miss Carter," he said with an enigmatic smile on his lips. "But in this case, it's out of necessity. If you can read between the lines, I know that you already have the information. Because I don't intend to reveal anything new to you, Miss Carter." Dropping his eyes to her full breasts for the first time, he added, "not without my payment."

"Fine," she said, ignoring how her nipples tightened and body was turning into a traitor that helped the enemy succeed. No! She would treat this like any other business negotiation and not let anything jeopardize her success, least of all her own body. Taking a calming breath she added, "I'll think about it and get back to you."

For a second he looked confused. Both knew that she'd already accepted his offer. Why stall? Sure, it was an unconventional deal but that didn't take away from the immense value he was offering: getting access to all the information she'd ever wanted about Kerry. Offering her body was a small price to pay. At least that's how Sofie rationalized it. It would only be a simple physical chore. Something necessary to reach a goal; like going for a jog on a rainy morning. Hell, the sun was out and there was a good chance she might even enjoy the exercise, so there was no need to procrastinate.

But it was her habit to sleep over any big decisions. And the ache between her legs warned her that she might indeed not be thinking very logically right now. So stalling was absolutely necessary. It would enable her to get over this intoxication she had for this man, who was as handsome as he was savvy.

"Miss Carter, I cleared my schedule for tonight. There is no need to wait."

How confident! He had been expecting her to take the deal. Was it because he thought himself too irresistible, or her too single-mindedly to delay gratification? Either way, it wasn't flattering and the worst thing was that he might even be right. Because there was something deeper than desire or curiosity that drew her in. Something that nagged her to throw caution into the wind. She sensed a kindred spirit in him that she found hard to resist.

His observational skills were as sharp as hers, perhaps sharper. A rare asset generally, and absolutely vital for an investigative journalist. She could picture herself working with him, side-by-side digging into cases. His charm and her logic, the perfect combination.

She pulled herself out of this daydream. It was far more likely that all of this was an elaborate web of lies; fabricated to dial up the heat-level and blind her to his real intentions. It could very well be a trap. Maybe he was working with MP Kerry after all. Or it was simply a game to keep him entertained. He could be toying with her, building her emotions up, until a carefully applied 'Our time is up, Miss Carter' brought everything crashing down when he's had enough.

"What's in it for you?" Sofie asked, not bothering to lower her voice this time.

Philip sat back, resting one leg leisurely on the other with the fine wool of his Italian designer pants accentuating his muscular calves. He studied her in silence. Was he miffed? If so, it wasn't because he was afraid of being discovered. He looked relaxed. In control. He let his foot sway in the air. The sole of his leather shoes were absolutely pristine and unscratched. They were either brand new or he indeed never left the softly carpeted mansion. Who was this man? What was his life like?

The metal clasps of his expensive silver timepiece jiggled as he checked the time. He was waiting for her to break the silence before their time was running out. But not this time. This time, she needed him to answer. She needed to know why he was doing this before she would even consider taking him up on his offer.

"Spending a night with a beautiful woman," he finally replied, "that's what's in it for me."

Yeah, right! Even if she was his idea of irresistible perfection, he wasn't the type to carelessly give into his desires. This man was a calculated creature of luxury. Wrapped in cotton wool by the carefully stacked layers of wealth and power inside the Club.

"That's what you think I want to hear?"

Of course he did. His horizon had shrunk to the inner world of Elandra. For Philip, only pleasure and games existed. He was so far removed from the struggles of the real world that he couldn't even comprehend the monstrosities MP Kerry would unleash on the world if elected PM.

"Yes, Miss Carter, I indeed think that's what you want to hear, whether you admit it or not. But..." He reached for her arm before Sofie could get up to leave in frustration, "what you should be hearing is that winter is coming. The Monach butterfly won't be beautiful when it migrates. And once it has moved up in the world, no one can reach it anymore. Who knows what laws it overthrows next."

Winter is coming? He was talking about the election. It was a mere 10 months away and once elected, MP Kerry had powers that made her untouchable. So he knew what electing her meant. Just like her, he was concerned about the absolute power Kerry was after.

"Yes, Philip. Time is running out! So stop playing games and give me what I need!"

Sofie's anger rolled off Philip like water off a lotus leaf.

"Miss Carter, you said my information is not for selfish reasons and I accept that you can't say more. That's why I've asked for a deed instead. It's the only thing I can verify in here and it speaks louder than words."

"I see," Sofie nodded, acknowledging the subcontext in his answer. He was a prisoner, trapped inside Elandra, without communication to the outside world. But that didn't suddenly make him trustworthy. If anything, there were more angles to consider. "And I'll get back to you with my decision."

He needed to see that their relationship was one of equals. She was as important to him as he was to her. He needed to stop dictating the terms, if he really wanted to stop Kerry.

But instead of caving he just smiled at her. Sofie had not expected that reaction.

"Well, you know where to find me, Miss Carter."

His tone was mischievous, it said 'Look who's making a game out of this now!'

It wasn't exactly a game to her but she indeed needed to take back control in whatever this was.

Done playing games

Sofie stood in the lobby of Club Elandra. It had been two weeks since she was here last. Even though she'd made her decision the very next day, it took this long to secure another visit. She clearly wasn't getting any special treatment, despite Philip stressing how little time there was left.

It probably was just a game, that's what her mind fell back on as the days were stretching in anticipation of tonight. It couldn't come soon enough. All this suspense, the excitement, the jitters, it wasn't normal. Nothing of this felt like her usual cases. It was like looking forward to... a date.

"How you've been?" she asked Melanie to take her mind off this incriminating yearning.

But the receptionist only shook her head and hastily reached for the phone to make the discrete call to Philip. Sofie took the hint, it was too dangerous to talk, even if no one was around. Instead, she adjusted her dress for the third time and glanced into the mirror above the side table. Yes, she was tense, but at least she looked good!

"Philip? Miss Carter is here for you."

It sounded harmless and professional, though to Sofie it felt anything but. Her palms were sweaty and her heart was beating in her throat. Was she really such a nervous wreck? The heck why? She had been in difficult situations before. Even life threatening ones. They never got to her. But tonight felt different. Tonight, she put herself in danger. Her heart was threatening to cut off her escape routes. If things got out of control this could spiral into an addiction. An addiction that would leave her craving for an obscenely priced drug she could never afford again.

She heard the familiar footsteps and her heart rate accelerated when Philip walked down the stairs. He wore his navy-blue suit and an enigmatic smile. Just like he did haunting her dreams, where she would slide her hand between the buttons of his white shirt to feel the warmth of his skin.

Sofie had never been the drug-seeking type; allowing herself pleasures only in carefully controlled quantities. But she was different with Philip. She couldn't trust herself around him. She wanted to taste the forbidden fruit. Lose her restraints. Take it all. She was curious, eager and reckless. And somehow, she was strangely ok with that.

"Welcome back to Club Elandra, Miss Carter."

"Good to be back."

Her voice sounded normal. As if this was a regular Thursday night for her. Good! At least some parts of her body were still under her control.

"Shall we?" he asked, holding out his hand.

Philip's eyes met Sofie's. A sharp pain shot through her belly, and she could only nod in response to his question. Her voice would surely betray her this time.

Keeping her cool was even harder than expected. Her nerves were meant to settle after seeing him in the flesh. After comparing the real Philip with the imaginary version she had unwittingly elevated to perfection in her head. After finding this one unsatisfactory. But to her dismay, he was just as handsome, just as intriguing, just as capable of reading her desires. And her pulse quickened realizing that the real Philip could even fulfil them.

She needed the short walk to his room to regain her equilibrium. Acclimate to his presence, to the instant electricity, and to that intoxicating scent of his.

Arriving at the bedroom suite was a deja-vu. Everything was as delectable and exclusive as she remembered. The only difference was an ice bucket with champagne instead of scotch on the coffee table.

"Do you want a glass?" he asked, not even offering alternatives.

It was a safe choice. One might call it the boring choice, if not for the infuriating fact that sparking wine was the only alcoholic drink Sofie actually enjoyed. He couldn't have known that. Could he?

"Yes, thank you."

She ignored the excitement she felt from the pop of the freshly opened bottle, and took a seat.

"So, you've decided to take me up on my offer."

His fingers touched hers as he handed her the champagne flute and seated himself beside her. She could feel the slight dip on the leather couch, it mimicked the emotional pull she already felt towards him.

"Why do you say that? I might still only want to talk."

She aimed for 'teasing confidence' but her tone betrayed her. She took a fidgety sip from the champagne glass. She had worked herself into a nervous wreck. The Sofie sitting on the couch tonight was a bundle of doubt and desire. A far cry from the cool and calculated journalist, she needed to be. She didn't even recognize herself. And she sure as hell did not like her. Maybe she should take the hint? Talking or, better yet, leaving sounded like the smart option all of a sudden.

"I don't think you wanted to talk," he smiled darkly. "You've made up your mind before you came."

"How'd you know?"

"You're wearing different makeup..." He lightly caressed her check with the back of his hand. Leaning closer to breathe her in, he added, "you put on perfume. And..." He traced two fingers across the shoulder straps of her bra. "You're wearing different underwear. Laces if I'm not mistaken." He chuckled. "And I can't wait to see what color."

He continued tracing her bra towards the middle of her chest, just where the lace ended and her skin began. Little goosebumps of pleasure followed his trail. Her body reacted even though he stayed well above the mount of her breasts, where her nipples had already formed hard aching buttons that tried to lure him in, like perilous sirens.

"But if you just want to talk." He moved back. "Then that's what we'll do."

"No."

She did not know where her conviction suddenly came from but she did not want his touch to end. Glancing into his eyes she saw a pure unbridled excitement, like he too needed this touch. It was there for only a fraction of a second before the sly mask of the controlled seducer fell back into place.

"But," she hedged, ignoring what she just saw, "I want to see the YubiKey first."

He leaned back, looking at her as if he could not quite connect her two opposing statements.

"Ever the player, Miss Carter!" He lightly shook his head, before adding with a chuckle, "for a moment, I thought we were finally done playing games."

Sofie breathed a sigh of relief. She managed to stay in control and her carefully crafted facade seemed to remain intact. She was still hiding the roaring fire within. A fire that rapidly cut off all her escape routes and trapped her inside her burning heart. But so far no one could see the state she was in, not even Philip.

To emphasize her point she replied, "I am never done playing, Philip. My work is too important."

"I see. Well then, the YubiKey is right over here."

He pointed to a stylish vitrine. Four glass walls formed a free standing multi-level tower. Like in a shrine, small light sources illuminated the delicate objects within. Sofie moved closer. There were little ceramic figurines, medals in their celebratory casings, and wooden sculptures. All unique, precious and likely irreplaceable. All belonging into a museum rather than the bedroom of a gigolo.

"What is all of this?" Sofie laughed. "Additional payments from your clients? Don't you think your horrendous price tag is more than enough already?"

Sofie's eye fell on the YubiKey. There were finely engraved red letters on the carbon black metal casing. The connecting gold circuits protruded from the main body. It looked delicate, intricate, and even smaller than a USB stick. Despite being a high-tech machine, it didn't look out of place amongst the other artefacts. For all intents and purposes it was just as valuable as the diamond crusted cup next to it. Perhaps even more so, for it had the power to change history.

Sofie's fingers twitched. It was right there! She could easily break the glass, take the key and run. But she wouldn't get very far. The security guards would have overpowered her long before she made it to her car. No. Honoring their deal was the only way. Was what separated her from what she wanted. So, she'd better get on with it.

But when she looked back at Philip his lips had turned into thin lines. He didn't like what she was implying about his price tag.

"They're tokens of appreciation," he said flatly. "It might seem strange to you, but some women enjoy spending time with me. They bring little souvenirs back to me, to let me know that they thought of me during their travels."

She swallowed. He didn't see his clients as cash cows. He formed a bond with them. It was more than just a service rendered. It was a sort of friendship. He treated them as human beings, while she was seeing him as a cliché only.

"I enjoy spending time with you too," she replied, glancing up at him. It was as close to an apology as she was willing to go.

With one fluid motion he closed the space between them and wrapped his arm around her waist.

"Then show me," he breathed against her lips.

He was waiting for her to take the lead. To initiate the kiss. His breathing had become shallow and Sofie could feel his heartbeat speeding up. Heat radiated from him. It hadn't been there before. The restraint to hold back was clearly costing him.

Sofie let her hand glide up his muscular arms, over the padded edges of his suit and embraced his broad shoulders. Electricity flowed through her body, as she connected with the skin above his starched collar. Warm and soft. Vulnerable. Inviting her in. This wasn't the gigolo. This was the man behind the myth. This was him.

She gently pulled his head closer and brushed her lips against his. The light flow of sparks turned into a ripping current as he kissed her back. His hand cradled the back of her head, fisting her long brown hair and their connection deepened. Desire swallowed Sofie and her hungry hands started to explore the rest of his body. A moan formed in her throat. Yes. This was what she needed and she wanted more. Wanted it all.

"Easy," he rasped, breaking away from her.

It wasn't clear whether he said it to her or himself. This kiss had affected him just as much, and clearly more than he had expected.

Sofie reached for her burning lips. Raw impulse had propelled her and she must have overstepped the mark. This was worse than what she had given herself concession for. It wasn't just curiosity and desire anymore. Looking into the fire burning unrestrained in his eyes, she knew that she had the ability to affect him too. This was a liability she could not allow herself. A slippery slope she was not prepared to navigate. This cannot go further.

Noticing the change, he let go of her and stepped back.

"You want out of our deal."

It wasn't a question. It was a statement. And he was reading her well. But it also carried an emotion that Sofie could not quite place. Unease? Frustration? Disappointment? Relief?

"You're very observant, Philip."

"It's my job to notice," he replied, deflated.

"Yes, but how?"

He sighed, humouring her by continuing the conversation.

"I use key principles from human psychology and deduce the likely outcome. Like, for example, that you like champagne. Or..." The energy in his voice suddenly changed, "that you still want the YubiKey. That the game is not over yet. You're hoping to renegotiate the terms. Am I right?"

"Impressive," Sofie mumbled, while racking her brain for the hint that had given away her intentions. "And yes, I've not given up."

"What makes you think I'm willing to change our deal?"

"Well Philip, I still have one more visit," she smiled with the confidence of knowing that she had finally taken control. "And I intend to make you an offer you'll find irresistible."

I accept your challenge

Sofie's cocky confidence took a dive when she realized that coming back with that 'irresistible' offer was harder than expected. She didn't know Philip or what his kryptonite could be. The only thing she was certain of: kissing him again was out of the question. She'd rather not have this skilled Mentalist command her every fantasy. This one kiss already stirred an addiction that could financially ruin her. No, what she needed was to dominate the situation and the shady plan she came up with was just the thing.

"Philip is coming downstairs to pick you up," the receptionist beamed.

It was a different person. Did Melanie finally manage to get away from this place? Sofie hoped so, though looking at the new receptionist, she felt a pang of sadness that yet another bright-eyed and bushy-tailed girl was pulled into this controlling society.

"Thank you," Sofie smiled back.

This time, she didn't feel nervous. This time, the plan put her in command of getting the YubiKey. She felt confident. Besides, this was her kind of work. Coming up with complex schemes and executing them perfectly. It's what she was good at. The more elaborate the better.

It was also necessary, because simply stealing the key in the dead of the night would not have worked. Club Elandra was like Fort Knox, located on a sprawling estate in the English countryside with patrolled fences and security cameras everywhere. Getting near it without an appointment was impossible. At least it was impossible for her, and involving more people introduced the kind of uncertainty that always led to failure.

She could have snatched the key during her visit. That would not have required to include anyone. Breaking into the flimsy vitrine would have been easy and quick. The only problem: Philip was always there, escorting her in and out, never leaving her out of sight. And he would call security if she tried anything. Of course, she could have spiked his drink with a laxative or narcotic, putting him out of action. But he likely had a panic button in the room and feeling that something was wrong he'd press it and the place would be crawling with guards before she could get to the key.

No, the only way to get the key was Philip giving it to her. It would have to be some sort of a trade. Like the one he offered, except this time it would be her bargaining chip. One that she was willing to give, yet it needed to be equally tempting to him. Luckily she found just the thing.

Waiting in the lobby, Sofie heard Philip's footsteps echo down the hall. She was excited about seeing him again. She spent the past two weeks thinking about him, not fantasizing about his body but focusing on his mind. What he liked, what motivated him, what type of deal would tempt him. She was keen to find out whether she'd been right and the plan would work on him.

She had to admit that finding the right bargaining chip was unusually difficult. He clearly wasn't enticed by the usual things: power and money. He had both in excess already. And their conversations had not given her much insight either, just a vague sense that under all the luxury and sexual confidence there was a decent person. Someone who wanted to do the right thing. Who realized Kerry was dangerous and was prepared to stop her.

The only thing she knew for sure was that Philip cared about his clients. Not in a business sense, but on an empathetic level. He felt protective enough to spell out what the souvenirs meant and defended the women and their choices. Could it be as simple as that? Find out which of his clients meant something to him and then use them as the bargaining chip?

Her plan was as straightforward as it was illegal. All she needed to do was spy on him interacting with his clients. Sofie was ok with the morally dubious aspect of it, she had done worse in the name of public good. The only thing giving her pause was having to watch Philip be with another woman. Giving her what she desired. Finding out exactly what she was missing out on. Sofie shook her head. It would be nothing more than watching a handsome actor in a raunchy love scene. Besides, there were bigger things to achieve here than her satisfaction.

Tonight she was planning to execute phase one of her plan: install the hidden cameras in the room of the world's most famous escort.

"Miss Carter, welcome to your fourth visit."

Philip's smile was charming and easy but there was something in his eyes that acknowledged that this was her last time.

"Great to be back, Philip."

This time, she did not have to fake self-assurance. She wasn't susceptible to the electricity he was already weaving between them. With satisfaction, she noticed that her newfound immunity took Philip aback.

"I have to admit," he opened the conversation when they arrived in his bedroom suite, "that I was surprised to see this as an 'in-room visit'. I thought you'd choose a more public setting... After last time."

Sofie considered meeting him at Elandra's restaurant. She expected that being with Philip would stretch her self-control to the limit. Having waiters whirling around them would certainly have helped. More importantly, meeting at the restaurant would have also meant his room was empty and she could have installed the cameras unseen. It was a good plan until she remembered how hushed Melanie was during her last visit. There were discreet security cameras mounted in the empty hallways, watching their every move. She would never have made it to his room undetected.

The plan she settled on instead was more subtle. It would convince him to leave the room. Using a pretence that was right up his alley.

"I decided to try again," she lied. "Last time, I wasn't quite ready. Not quite... turned on."

Philip's brow twitched. He wasn't buying this at all. Saying to him that she wasn't turned on was like telling an expert craftsman he had been using the wrong tools. He could tell she was lying. But he did not reply. Instead he waited for her to elaborate, to stumble over her own lies.

"Otherwise," she persisted, "I wouldn't have walked out on you. Wouldn't you agree?"

It was a challenge, like pointing out a rough edge on an artisan furniture. It was the dare for a craftsman to lift his game. And seeing the fire in his eyes, she knew he had taken the bait.

"Well, it certainly was a first for me," he volunteered, adding with a playful tone, "I'm glad you decided to give me another chance."

He moved closer, but Sofie held up a hand to stop him.

"I brought a vibrator," she said bluntly.

"Ok... That's another first."

The inflection in his voice made it sound like a question rather than agreement. Bringing a vibrator without discussing it with him was a blatant non-confidence vote on his skills. It hurt his professional pride. He clearly had a far higher opinion of himself and his competencies.

"The vibrator isn't for me," she corrected his assumption.

She pulled out a box from her bag and handed it to him.

"The Spaceship Pulse 2000," he read from the box's description, "is a small vibration toy, hugging him in all the right places. Designed to enhance solo flights or..." A mischievous twinkle came into his eyes. "Couples' playtime by..."

"Stop reading."

This was harder than expected. She wasn't quite sure anymore how she'd pictured him to react but treading it out like that wasn't her idea of fore-play. And neither was it his. No. This was a power play, aimed at making her feel uncomfortable and taking away her command on the situation.

"Miss Carter, this was your idea," he said with a mock complaint before softening his tone. "Hey, no need to be embarrassed. I'm happy to explore whatever it is you like."

He moved closer to brush a stray strand of hair behind her ear. "Though I have to admit that you look awfully cute with your flushed cheeks..."

"I don't want to use it with you," she said ignoring his offhanded compliment, "I want you to wear it under your clothes. While we talk... and I hold the remote control."

He paused, taking in the sharpness in her command. He just realized that it wasn't embarrassment that was painted across her face, it was... her temper.

"I didn't place you as a sadist, Miss Carter."

She lifted her chin defiantly and stood her ground. She could be whatever it took to get to her goal.

"Fine then," he smirked, "I accept your challenge. Let's see who wants to stop talking and abandon this game first. Because I don't think it'll be me."

Relief flooded Sofie as he headed to the bathroom to put on the device. Her plan had worked. As soon as the door closed behind him she jumped to action. Install the cameras and get out of here. This was more than enough acting for one night.

Sofie hastily looked around Philip's room to find the perfect location for installing them. The cameras were barely larger than a button, perfect for blending into the decor of the room. With state-of-the-art lenses and microphones, as well as a mobile connection, they would send the confidential information directly to her computer. And their tentacle-like cords would wrap around power cables of other electronic devices, keeping them operational indefinitely.

Sofie's heart beat like a war-drum, flooding her body with adrenaline. This was the excitement she liked. The kick she craved. She placed the first camera on the built-in shelf facing the lounge area. It was the higher resolution camera, which would be able to record the whole room as well as zoom into the private conversations on the sofa. With steady hands she wrapped its tentacle around the power cable of the stereo. Stepping back she evaluated her work. Perfect! The camera was hardly visible even when knowing exactly where it was.

A sudden buzz from the bathroom startled her. Philip was testing out the gadget and she could hear its vibrations through a closed bathroom door. She almost felt sorry for him. The things she could do to him, holding the remote. A damp hotness spread between her legs. Stop it. There will be none of this! You'll be out of here before.

Indeed, her plan was to leave straight after installing the cameras. She would say how embarrassing this all was and that they should forget this stupid deal. Knowing how easily he backed off last time, he probably wasn't too keen on actually handing over the YubiKey. So he probably wouldn't object to giving up altogether.

This would leave Sofie to start on phase two of her plan: collect intel to use against him. She smiled. He won't know what hit him, when she'll come back to him with the new terms of their deal.

Another buzz from the bathroom reminded her how little time there was left to install the second camera. He'd be putting his clothes back on soon. Quietly she padded to the entrance area and placed the second camera facing the door. It was only a low resolution camera but sufficient for recording who came in and out of his room. The hallway table with its standing light was almost too convenient for providing the disguise and power supply.

She was wrapping the tentacles around the power cable when the bathroom door opened. Sofie wheeled around.

"What are you doing in the hallway? Are you sneaking out on me?"

"Why would I?" She carefully hid how startled she really was. "Hand me the remote and let the games begin."

Offence was the best defence. She could not risk him getting suspicious about her standing in the entrance hall. What's the harm in playing, anyways? It would only be for a little while. Besides, leaving after she'd actually tried it was way more believable.

"Yes, Ma'am."

He handed her the little black remote. It had a curious weight to it; all its temptations felt heavy in her hand. Her fingers itched to press the button.

She wanted to make the famous escort squirm, lose his cool, surrender his control to her.

She felt her cheeks flush, this time with excitement.

It was playtime!

I have no control with you

W hy was Sofie still in Philip's room, holding the vibrator's control? The hidden cameras were placed and she was supposed to be out of here long ago. But she had to improvise when Philip snuck up on her in the hallway. She needed to think on her feet and going along with Philip's dare was the best diversion she could come up with. At least that's what she told herself. Of course, there was no way she would actually be playing, let alone caving in from desire as he predicted. The vibrator was her weapon and she would wield it wisely. Everybody knew that the odds were stacked against Philip. Unless, of course, he was not playing fair.

"Did you really put the vibrator on? For all I know, you'd left it in the bathroom and are just pretending."

"Press the button and find out."

It was a taunt, an invitation, a command. Their interaction had been theoretical for far too long and he clearly was keen to finally unleash his skills.

With a tentative smile, Sofie pressed the button and the little machine purred to life. He leaned back looking utterly relaxed as if nothing was amiss. While for Sofie, the mere thought of what the vibration did to him sent an arrow straight to her core. She realized that the odds against him were not quite as high as she initially thought.

She reminded herself that she wasn't actually playing and if she was, there were still four more vibration strengths to go. This was definitely his game to lose.

"Are you now convinced I am playing fairly?" he asked with a slight nod.

"Yes," she reluctantly admitted.

Just because he could hold it together for now does not mean anything!

"Then, how about you put some skin in the game too, Miss Carter?"

"What? That wasn't the deal!"

"Come on. You're making this way too easy for me. I can see that this already affects you more than me. At least, give me a challenge."

How could he be so unaffected by the machine between his legs? Even his observational skills were as sharp as ever. This hasn't been going well for Sofie so far.

"Fine! What are you suggesting?" she hedged.

"Unbutton your blouse for me."

What was he getting at? Did he really want to see her naked or was he counting on her feeling helpless without her clothes? This wasn't a game of strip poker and she wasn't a teenager. His strategy would fail and that suited Sofie just fine.

"Ok. But for every request I'll increase the vibration strength."

"Deal."

He smiled victoriously as he dropped his gaze to her neckline in anticipation. Did he see the hammering of her pulse? The light shake of her hands? Don't get self conscious! One by one Sofie opened the buttons of her silk blouse. The little plastic disks made a small popping sound as they slipped through the whole of the fabric. When she popped the last button she traced her fingers up the middle of her stomach to her breastbone. She moved the fabric to the side to reveal herself to him. Her full breasts tightly caged in the black lace bra that Philip wanted to see during her last visit. She knew how visible her nipples were in the sheer material and felt them hardening under his gaze. Squeezing her legs together she tried to curb the ache that was building up inside of her.

A sharp breath escaped from Philip's parted lips. She was turning him on! Her game was actually working!

"I take it I've levelled the playing field?"

"That you have, Miss Carter," he replied, dragging his eyes reluctantly away from her exposed cleavage.

"So is this how it usually goes? With your clients?"

"No," he laughed, genuinely amused. "No one ever dared me to finish before them. It's certainly not what anyone would pay money for."

"Of course..." she replied, feeling foolish.

To recover, she slipped into her journalist's mindset and asked "Having this level of control over your body is like being an elite athlete, is it not? You must have trained to build up stamina and will-power to succeed in this..." She paused, struggling to find an appropriate analogy, "game of endurance. When was the last time you played just for fun?"

"Is this a diversion, Miss Carter? Making small talk because you feel yourself caving in already?"

He nodded towards the large double-bed with a taunting smile.

"Are you afraid to answer my question, Philip? Sounds like you're diverting yourself."

"No... " He straightened himself. "I admit it's been a while since I did this... for fun. Probably years."

His answer was slow and his focus drifted. He was contemplating the ramifications. For a journalist this was a tell-tale sign, like blood in the water for a shark. It told her to circle. To attack. To sink her teeth deeper into this juicy story.

"You're surrounded by beautiful women, yet you tell me that you haven't been tempted in years?"

"It's not as surprising as you think."

"Why?"

"I'm not attracted to my clients."

Disappointment struck Sofie out of nowhere. She was his current client. If he wasn't attracted to her, then why was she even playing? She suddenly felt like trying to best a master in a game where she didn't even know the rules.

"It's different with you," he added as if he sensed her struggle. "I don't know what to make of you... And that's why, you should take off your pants so we can find out together."

Smooth. Sofie had to smile. Philip managed to playfully stir the conversation back on point. His point, mind you.

"Is that so?" Relief and excitement formed a strange and intoxicating cocktail that she found herself drinking up all too eagerly, wanting to see where this was going. "So? I take it, you're ready for the next vibration level?"

He nodded with a confidence that set every competitive fibre in Sofie's body ablaze. She stood up, her hands slowly sliding down the zipper of her pants. She unfastened the button of her black dress pants. And with one elegant shimmy the fabric coast off her hips and pooled at her feet.

Philip lightly sucked his lower lip between his teeth as he moved his eyes along her long graceful legs. He was taken in by the moment, not aware of what he was doing or how his small gesture brought a hot flush to Sofie's cheeks.

Triumphantly, she sat back down to meet his eyes. To her surprise, he looked back at her with a neutral expression. How could he have regained his control so quickly? Luckily, Sofie was not done yet. With a sinful smile she lightly spread her thighs, exposing her black laced panties and the translucently clothed vee between her legs. Before Philip had time to adjust to the sight, she hit the button to increase the vibration strength.

His cheek muscles tightened and his breathing increased. Yes, this finally started to have an effect on him.

"Miss Carter," he rasped, "You know how to play."

But even with all this, it took him much less time to regain his equilibrium than Sofie had expected. And with a dark grin he was ready to issue his next request.

"I want you to touch yourself."

"Next level already? Are you sure?" she countered.

"No."

His reply was quick. Was this finally a sign of weakness?

"You'll give me this one for free... because, Miss Carter, you know you want it more than me."

It was true. The ache between her legs had become painful and throbbing. She was dying to stroke the overheating flesh to ease the sensation. But was it strong enough to lose the game? Certainly not!

"Rarely anything in life is free, Philip. You of all people should know that. If you want me to find relief, you need to pay. Let's see how altruistic your request really was."

He closed his eyes and let a hand run through his light brown hair. When he opened them again the heat on his skin had recited. Whatever dark voodoo he conjured up worked. He looked as calm and relaxed as he was at the beginning of the night.

"If that's what it takes, I am ready to pay the sacrifice."

Dammit! There must be a limit to his self-control! Let's find it!

Sofie slipped her hand between the elastic of her panties, sliding down to where the storm raged. A small sigh escaped her lips as she stroked between the folds, smoothing out the aching cramps.

"Keep going."

His voice was dark and suggestive, tempting her to go further, to climb higher. She dipped her fingers into the warm wetness and a moan wrangled free from her lips. She had to remind herself that this was war. That his erection was her weapon and that she could not lose her edge.

She pulled her hand back. With dark calculation she slowly licked her arousal from her glittering fingers. The effect on Philip was immediate and devastating. She almost felt sorry for pressing the button of the remote control at this very moment.

He grabbed the armrest of his chair, his fingers pressing into the soft leather. A low rumble came from his throat. Was it pleasure or agony? Likely both. He was losing the control he had cultivated for years. He hurled himself forward and snatched the remote out of her hands. With a tortured look he switched off the device.

"Enough!" he gasped.

Sinking back into his chair, his chest heaved rapidly as he was catching his breath. "I never climax with clients. And certainly not like this." Avoiding her gaze he added, "This isn't what I wanted."

Sofie could not help but feel for the man who puts his partners before him. Who placed himself in a vulnerable position for her. Who stopped the game before it got out of hand.

"What do you want?" she asked slowly.

But as the silence stretched, doubts suddenly festered in her mind. Had he been planning this? Make her care for him? Get under her skin? Set her up for the final strike? She never checked if this was real, after all. If he rigged the game. If he truly was wearing the device or whether he was a terrific actor.

She closed the distance between them. Leaning over him she anchored herself with one hand on the back of his chair, while letting the other drop to his leg.

He closed his eyes and inhaled sharply, savouring her touch, her nearness. As she moved up his thigh, his expression suddenly hardened.

"You're only doing this because you don't trust me," he said, opening his eyes, her face only inches from his. "Go on, then. Find out what you wanted to check."

Holding his stare, her fingers moved up to find the hard shell of the machine. It had not been an act. She had been in the wrong.

A twinge of remorse made her hesitant to pull back and something in his glare dared her to not part just yet. She let her hand explore further. It was impossible to tell where the machine ended and he began. Everything she touched was hard and unmoving. But she must have found his flesh, because his breathing had become rapid.

"Stop."

The sharpness in his voice made her jump. Leaning forward to breathe her in, he added softly, "I cannot do this. I have no control with you."

His confession felt like a hot dagger to her centre, making it impossible to resist him any longer.

"What if I don't want to stop?"

Her question evaporated the darkness in his eyes.

"Only one way to keep this going," he smiled. "You had your hands on me. What do you say, Miss Carter? Are you granting me the same privileges? Fair is fair?"

That's when Sofie realized that she won the fight, but lost the war. She now wanted him more than the YubiKey and the anticipation was killing her.

"Yes. I want to see what you can do."

I want you to touch me

Reckless, that's what she was right now! Why would she give Philip permission to touch her? But then again, what's wrong with living a little? Ever since meeting Philip she was ready to throw caution and discipline out the window to be careless and free if only for just one night.

Philip rose from his armchair. Like a panther approaching a mate, there was danger crackling in the air. His muscles flexed and his eyes locked on hers. He knew exactly what he was doing and Sofie's breathing increased as he approached. It was like sitting in a roller-coaster cart; slowly climbing to the top. Ra-ta-ta-ta-taaa. The thrill was inevitable. She had already committed to it. But was she looking forward to it? Or was it just too risky after all?

Her heart raced as she watched Elandra's most handsome and experienced escort sink to his knees in front of her. His face was inches from her's. She could feel his breath on her skin, minty and warm. Instinctively she closed her eyes and leaned in. Her body treacherously betrayed the burning desires within. There was only so much self control to go around and she yearned for him, ever since their first kiss. Her lips burned in anticipation of his touch.

But the touch never came. He did not kiss her. His lips only lightly brushed her cheekbones and hovered over her ear.

"I have other plans", he whispered, his words tingling the sensitive skin of her earlobes and sending shivers down her spine.

He positioned himself between her legs and slipped his hands under her thighs. With one firm tuck he slid her body towards him until their middles met. The sudden movement drew a small gasp from Sofie's lips but quickly transformed into a soft moan as their groins connected. She could feel his hard length and the vibrator that was still wrapped around it.

Steadying herself, she rested her hands on his forearms. When she looked up, his eyes met hers. His liquid honey melted in her green emeralds and the world started to fall away around her. Nothing else existed as she let her hands slide down his flanks, feeling the strong muscles that connected his broad torso to his waist.

Despite the fabric between them, his body felt as intimate and exciting as if she was touching his bare skin. She leaned forward to give her hands more room to explore. This subtle shift in posture pressed her soft breasts against his chest and he inhaled sharply at the sudden sensation. Even with the ball firmly in her court and facing an experienced player, there was power in her actions. Encouraged by this, she moved her fingers down to his buttocks and traced the pronounced dimples on each side. It felt firm and round under her palms. He growled in objection as the member between his legs twitched to life.

Instead of pulling back, he started his own offence: he opened her legs further and trailed along her inner thigh with the back of his hand. Heat spread along the path and carried forward like embers in a wildfire, setting her sex ablaze.

She let go of his body to lean back and savour the sensation. A small part of her acknowledged his skilful manipulation, but the rest of her decided it did not matter. The rest just wanted to dive head first into the wave, crashing over her as his fingers reached the epicentre of her desire. She moved her hips forward to give him better access.

He lightly brushed across the flimsy black fabric that separated her burning flesh from his touch. She could feel the warmth of his hands teasing and leaving her wanting for more. But he made no attempts to take it further. He just lightly brushed across the lace of her panties, creating small torturous vibrations. It was like eating fairy floss where every endorphine-triggering bite melts away into nothing.

"I want you to touch me," she bit out.

A victorious smile crossed his lips as he finally pushed the fabric to the side and let his meticulously manicured fingers glide through her folds. Her intense wetness instantly reduced the friction of his skin, making his touch furiously unsatisfying. As if he could read her mind he wiped his fingers on the inside of his palm. An unbridled moan tumbled from her lips, as his dryer fingertips created just the amount of pressure she needed to make her nerves explode with pleasure. Within seconds he had her climbing to precarious heights.

"You are so responsive," he mumbled in wonder.

His touch was paced to make her soar but not to find her release. She was floating at an unfamiliar altitude and her body was so charged with electricity that the muscles inside her cramped from the absence of a lighting rod.

"I need more," she rasped.

He slipped a finger inside her warm wetness. It was less than she wanted but enough to reduce the aching need within. He let his finger move in and out, pressing his palm firmly against her pleasure centre at the end of every stroke. He knew exactly how to make her body sing and it seemed so effortless for him.

"Yes... like... that. I'm close."

He slowed the pace.

"Not yet, there is so much more I want to show you".

Sofie expected sex with him to be great, but this was more than she'd bargained for. If this was only a fraction of his expansive repertoire she could see how a night with him turned into a never ending hunger in his clients.

"No, keep going," she insisted; no need to venture further into the forbidden forest.

His nostrils flared. He obviously wanted more time with her. He was not ready to end it just yet. Why wasn't he treating her like a regular client? Or was he doing just that? Ensuring, she would be hooked, that she would be coming back for more. He let his eyes glide over her: Her palms against the leather couch, pressing herself into his touch; her back arched from the desire ricocheting in her body; her eyes closed and her lips wet. Despite being rattled by the intensity of her emotions, he could see that had not gotten her to the point of no return. It would take a lot more to reel her in. She wasn't one of his typical clients. There was an unfamiliar complexity to her.

He shut his eyes and exhaled. Was he disappointed? Conflicted? Whatever it was it only lasted for a second before he followed through with her command. He steadily picked up the pace, circling his fingers against the spot he knew would tip her over the edge efficiently. Her moans got louder and shivers rolled through her body as the climax finally took her.

Slowly Sofie floated back to earth. She opened her eyes to find Philip still kneeled between her open legs. He smiled and his handsome face was slightly flushed. The magnitude of the quake he unleashed in her had affected him too. The vibrator was only a passing freight train in comparison. Sofie wondered what the aftermath would look like if they actually gave into this earth shattering passion of theirs. She suddenly wanted to find out, and felt the sharp claws of a budding addiction sink into her mind.

"Thank you, for..." She paused, unsure what to call the intimacy they just shared.

He took his seat, launching against the chair as if nothing unusual had taken place between them. He feels nothing! It was just a service for him!

"My pleasure, Miss Carter."

Clean and distant. Just like he was trained.

All the emotion, the attraction, the lust she read into his response had just been in her head, or worse, was a carefully performed act. She could feel the claws rip through her flesh as she tried to banish the thoughts of how good his body felt near hers, and how much she wanted to lean forward and kiss him right now.

Luckily, this was her last visit and she did not have the means to pay for more. Sampling his wares, if ever so briefly, had already set unrealistic standards for her future but at least it was a craving that could still be controlled.

She cleared her throat. She wasn't here for fairytale endings, anyways, but to do a job.

"So? Where is the YubiKey?"

He laughed at the sudden change in her demeanor. He leaned forward to ask, "Have you held up your end of the bargain, Miss Carter?"

"Yes!"

Ignoring her conviction, he crooked his head as if to say 'are you sure'.

"It was close enough, wasn't it? Wasn't my fault that you wanted to cut your part short."

She could not keep the sour tone out of her voice. It dampened her mood already that he made her feel things she had not felt in years, was he now also going to get petty about the specifics what constitutes sex?

"'Close enough' doesn't count in my profession, Miss Carter. And I gather neither does it in yours." A sharpness crept into his voice. "You wanted to use the vibrator to shortcut our agreement."

"I wasn't..." Sofie defended herself, but realized how futile the discussion was. "Look, you wanted to share information. Didn't you? And I even think you need to, because deep down you know that keeping them secret is wrong. So, let's be reasonable here and help each other out."

"What's right and wrong is rarely absolute, Miss Carter. It depends entirely on context and point of view. So, I don't need to share anything." He swallowed. He was annoyed. "I don't know what you think of me and what I do. But I like my life. And I don't think there is anything wrong with it. I get to talk to interesting accomplished women every day. My job pays well. And I am good at what I do."

He was more than 'good', Sofie could still feel the endorphins circulating her body despite this sudden and unfortunately turn in their conversation.

"Handing over information to you," he continued, "would jeopardize all of this. And so far, you haven't given me anything to build trust. So, I think what's needed here is for you to share some information first."

The truth of his statement hung heavy in the air. She was not used to dealing with informants that were her equal in scheming and deception. She never had to build true trust before. Nor did she have to argue about the shades of gray of moral decision making. Her usual cases were clear cut: innocent people were murdered or the law was broken for treacherous greed. High-politics seems to be playing by different rules. Vigilantism on a war-criminal who kept evading justice wasn't so easy to judge anymore and neither was greed for the good of a country. That's exactly why Sofie needed to get all the facts about Kerry's crimes, figuring out which shade of wrong she fell on and cut off her options to scheme her way back to white.

"You could start by telling me who you work for," Philip suggested.

He obviously still considered working with her. But he was not desperate or naive enough to trust just anyone. He was extending an olive branch but Sofie remained silent. This was unfamiliar territory for her, she needed to be careful. One wrong step and her morally gray actions could be exposed too.

"Who are you? What are your goals? C'mon, it's ok to open up, you can trust me..."

Sofie smiled. Trust actually goes both ways. And so far, this gigolo had not convinced her that treating him as an equal was beneficial or necessary either. After all, she had a plan in place that did not require any cooperation from him.

She stood and extended her hand.

"Well, Philip, it seems we'll not be working with each other, after all."

Philip's face fell. He wasn't used to receiving hard-nosed responses like this, especially ones he did not even see coming.

Philip was still searching for words, when Sofie left his room. She could not wait to log into the security cameras to watch the fallout of her dramatic exit. She only hoped that he would not skip his evening engagement because of it, even if seeing him be with another woman made a small part of her scream with jealousy. But at least she would find out his weakness and with it Kerry's secrets.

The woman I desire

S ofie rejected Philip's olive branch. She did not need to build trust, all she needed was leverage. It's better to be feared than loved; it yields more consistent results. And with the hidden cameras placed in Philip's suite, coming across the right leverage was only a matter of time. That is, if they worked.

As soon as Sofie arrived back at her car she pulled out her phone to dial up the cameras. She stared anxiously at the black screen, while the dial was spinning to establish the connection. What if they didn't work? What if she did something wrong in her haste to install them? It would have all been for nothing! Worse, she would lose access to Philip for good. The thought of never talking to him again made her heart flutter, for more than just her professional reasons. Stop it right there! As a cold-blooded journalist, she relied on facts and technology. Emotions were an unnecessary distraction. As if to confirm her credibility and conviction, the camera connected and the screen came to life.

Music filled the inside of Sofie's car. Her phone was the window into Philip's room, and it relayed Damien Rice's voice singing 'No love, no glory. No hero in her skies'.

Philip was sitting in his armchair, swirling a brandy in his hand. He stared at the couch on which Sofie had moments ago experienced pure euphoria.

Log out! Philip's night is starting soon and you've got a long drive ahead of you.

Her thumb hovered over the disconnect button. But for some reason she found it difficult to let go. She could still feel his hands weaving their magic across her body. And she wanted to relive the feeling for just a moment longer.

The cameras are working, god dammit. No need to dwell.

The song continued, 'I can't take my eyes off you', as Sofie watched Philip take another sip of brandy and lean back. He rolled his head to the side and massaged the back of his neck; there was a tension in him that Sofie could feel all the way out to the parking lot. He was contemplating something.

Don't go there. Whatever he is thinking about is not your problem!

With a sigh Sofie pressed the dial-out button, just as the string instruments cut to their solo. She had to leave now if she wanted to be home in time for Philip's evening engagement.

She was already cutting it fine and the unusually bad traffic made her even later. All the way from the highway exit to her home she anguished over missing the talking part of the evening and logging into finding Philip and his client in bed already.

She slammed the front door shut, kicked off her shoes and connected to the hallway camera, just in time to see Philip walking in. He had changed into formal attire. A black suit, white shirt, buttoned up to the top, sharp and crisp. He looked exquisite and Sofie felt a little breathless. Or was that from running up two flights of stairs?

He would have been appropriately dressed for the opera or a gala dinner, yet all this splendor was to entertain the beautiful woman by his side. She was in her forties. An elegant white silk dress flowed over her long legs, and a low cut back revealed her toned body. Philip touched the small of her back as she walked through the door, lightly stroking her bare dusk-colored skin. She flicked her wavy black hair and smiled at him as soft piano music played from the bedroom. This scene could not have been more perfect if it was designed for a romantic bollywood movie.

Sofie's lips turned into a thin line. They looked absolutely stunning together. And even worse, she recognized the woman. It was Ms Hunt, a second generation Briton from Indian descent and the youngest CEO to run a $30 billion insurance company. She was rich, successful and ... not married.

"He plays music for her! He never did that for you!" a sore little voice whined in her head. With a firm shake she reminded herself that this was a job and that Philip's only value was as her informant.

Sofie switched over to the second camera in the bedroom. The higher resolution camera filled her whole screen and showed their faces in brilliant detail. Ms Hunt looked relaxed and happy. It was an intimate glimpse at the private person behind the stern and perpetually annoyed businesswoman the media portrayed her to be.

"What would you..."

Philip stopped mid-sentence and looked up. There was a puzzled look on his face. He must have noticed something? But what? The camera was well hidden. His eyes scanned across the wall shelf, swiping across the camera several times before finally stopping and glaring at Sofie straight through the lense of her spy cam. Her heart stopped.

He spotted the camera! How did he do that?

With an annoyed expression he walked straight to the shelf and reached out.

Oh, No, No, No, No.

But instead of grabbing the camera, his hand reached for the volume dial of the stereo.

"Sorry, the music was a bit loud," he explained before turning to the mini-bar and pouring Ms Hunt a glass of red wine. "So, how was your royal commission hearing today? Did it go well?"

"How sweet of you to remember," Ms Hunt beamed. She seemed genuinely delighted by Philip's interest in her life. "Yes, it went very well actually. They were good, I have to give them that. Came prepared with some hard questions." With a triumphant smile she sank onto the couch. "But I was better."

"What do you mean 'better'?"

"Well, they obviously were out to expose the skeletons in our closets," she laughed, "Everybody knows that to outwit the banks you have to bend a rule or two. But they couldn't prove any of it!"

Sofie's journalistic bones itched; she could already see the headline: Fortune 500 CEO confesses to illegal practices. Philip would be a true treasure trove, if only he talked to her. Once he talked, she corrected herself with a smile.

"We've been doing this for 25 years," Ms Hunt continued, "and our official books are solid. So the only way they would have gotten evidence is through internal informants. But I tied everyone down good," she grinned as she slipped out of her shoes and placed a beautifully manicured foot on Philip's thigh. "Including you."

He took her foot and gently started massaging her sole.

"That you have, Ms Hunt," he said, adding in a lower tone, "in more ways than one."

"Yes, and I still cannot believe my luck."

Ms Hunt pressed a hand over her eyes, smiling at him from under her lowered gaze. What was she doing? Was she being shy?

"I feel the same," he breathed, gliding his hands up her leg.

The woman who braved a royal commission without batting an eyelid, started blushing and giggling like a schoolgirl. How is this possible? What kind of witchcraft is he practicing?

"Let's say we move this along," she exhaled, sliding along the sofa to his side.

"You had a hard day today," he replied, standing up before she could touch him, "how about, I give you a show."

"Oh, I like the sound of that."

She leaned back and took a sip of her wine.

"And I like having the eyes of the woman I desire on me," he smiled while slipping out of his jacket.

Sofie could not help but feel excited too. She'd wondered one too many times how he looked without his shirt. She zoomed the camera in on Philip, giving her an even better view than Ms Hunt. He unfastened the buttons of his white shirt, one by one, revealing his muscular torso. As the smooth fabric slipped off his shoulders, Sofie's fingers twitched. She yearned to run her hand over his perfectly groomed chest. It looked silken and smooth, with just enough hair to accentuate his sculpted pecs and form a hint of a line running from his navel to his belt.

Sofie's breath caught. It's been hours, but she could still smell his scent and feel the ghost of his fingers pleasuring her. How could he have such a command over her body, from miles away and while being with another woman.

As if he could hear her thoughts he looked at the camera and gave it a wink. After a blur of motion Sofie's monitor cut to white and the speakers emitted a loud rustling noise. With shock Sofie realized that Philip had covered the camera with his shirt and was ripping it off its powersource.

With one final crack the screen turned black, displaying 'connection lost' in bright red letters across her monitor and Sofie found herself back in her room. Sitting alone in the dark. Still wearing her outdoor jacket and holding her car keys. In stunned silence, she let sink in what just happened.

He obviously had spotted the camera and wasn't just adjusting the volume. From then on it had all been an act. For her. But what was his message?

I like having the eyes of the woman I desire on me.

With slightly trembling fingers Sofie logged into the hallway camera, secretly hoping he would evict Ms Hunt and talk to her.

The woman I desire. Sofie wanted that to be her. But as the minutes stretched without activity in the hallway she scolded herself for having even gone there. Just like she wasn't willing to jeopardize her success at work, neither was he.

Sofie got up from the chair and finally took off her jacket. With one eye on the screen she fixed herself dinner. She got half way through her bland cauliflower gratin when Philip re-appeared on the screen. He walked to the door before stopping dead in his tracks and letting his eyes swipe over the hallway furniture.

No! Not the second camera as well.

"What's wrong?" Ms Hunt's soft voice came from off-screen.

Philip focused back on her to smile his warm honeydew smile.

"Something feels different here," he said almost absentmindedly while giving the hall one last aimless swipe.

"I'll tell you what's different..." Stepping into the scene, Ms Hunt placed her slender hand on his cheek. "It was you. You were absolutely spectacular tonight."

She reached up to pull him into a long kiss.

Sofie's stomach tightened. Seeing him actually be intimate with another woman made her lose all appetite. She pushed her dinner away. This could be a hungry couple of weeks, if she felt like this with all of his engagements.

"I didn't think sex with you could get any better," Ms Hunt breathed, "but seeing you being lost in your release adds a whole new dimension. And I really like it. Next time, let's do it again. That way you can practice calling my name," she laughed, adding with a wink, "though, I don't mind being Sofie, if you make it up to me like that every time."

Excuse me, what was that? Did she hear that right? He called out her name while having sex with Ms Hunt? This was getting more twisted by the minute. And judging by how uncomfortable Philip looked, this wasn't one of his carefully planned manipulations.

"We'll see about that, Ms Hunt." Philip guided her out the door while placing a small kiss on her shoulder. "For now, I am looking forward to our date in 2 weeks. I've booked Elandra's restaurant for our regular time."

"Actually, Philip, I'm feeling adventurous. I think I want to be seen with you. After all this bad press, I deserve a bit of self-adulation. You know, having some envious eyes on me. So how about we go to the city instead.

There is this new restaurant everyone talks about. It's at West End... out of all places... and absolutely ..."

The rest of their conversation was cut off by the door closing behind them.

Sofie disconnected the camera. She was disappointed. Overall, tonight was a bust: she lost the main camera before learning anything relevant. While Ms Hunt had dodgy business practices, she was clearly not the leverage Sofie needed to get Philip talking. At least there was one camera left and a whole register of clients for Philip to go through. Time to call it a night and go to bed.

In the dark of her room, pictures of Philip calling out her name in ecstasy flooded her mind and she drifted off to sleep with a smile on her lips.

A persistent buzzing brought her reluctantly back. Her phone on the side table was brightly illuminated. Someone was calling. She groaned and groggily reached for the device, ready to turn it off. But reading the number on the display, she suddenly was wide awake. It was the camera's SIM card.

How could it be calling her? Who was calling her?

You turn me on

After spying on Philip, Sofie fell asleep disappointed and confused. He destroyed her main camera, stopping her from collecting more intel, but he also called out her name while being with another woman. It either was a ruthless ploy to get back at her for bugging his room or this conscience-proof gigolo had feelings for her. It was twisted, either way. But what's even more twisted: her phone was ringing with her spy cam's number.

"Miss Carter...," Sofie instantly recognized Philip's voice on the other end. It was deep and low, creating an intimacy that matched her cosy dark bedroom.

"You took it to the next level," he continued.

He didn't sound angry. Instead, there was a weariness in his voice, like he was over playing games.

"Philip," she rasped, still groggy from waking up. "How did you get this number?"

"That's your response? Ok. I see the gloves have come off." He paused, he needed to decide how to handle this, "I took your camera apart and found the SIM. This was the last number on the card."

Damit! Her computer dialed in with an untraceable connection, but her mobile had simply called the SIM. She had been careless in her haste to find out whether the cameras worked.

"How did you spot the camera?"

"Ha, Miss Carter, you continue to underestimate me." Underneath the mockery, Sofie heard a different emotion. Was it hurt? Perhaps disappointment that Sofie didn't give him credit for his unusual talent to notice the strange, the hidden, the secret. "The stereo sounded odd. It was only for a second. But it's never happened before and today I noticed it twice. First a couple of minutes after you left and then again when I got back with my client. So, I had a look and there it was."

The cameras created a small power-surge when switched on. It was only for a split second and hardly noticeable. But apparently obvious enough for Philip's uncanny senses.

"How did you know it was me?"

"No one else would dare."

There was a sharpness in his voice that made Sofie's blood run cold. Was he showing who he really was under all the suave polished veneer?

"Why are you calling, Philip?"

"I think I've given you the wrong impression. You don't seem to realize how powerful Elandra is and what a dangerous game you are playing here."

Sofie didn't respond to his blunt warning. She leaned back into her plush pillows. Feeling the warmth from where she had been sleeping before. This time, she was comfortable with the silence, with where the conversation was going, with what he implied.

No one dared taking them on. Until now. It gave her a smug satisfaction. She would be the first to conquer this mountain. It's what she did: taking down the institutions that were too big to fail, too scrupulous to yield, too dangerous to bring to justice. These David-and-Goliath fights were her speciality.

"Are there any more cameras?" Philip continued his interrogation undeterred. "Because if there are, you better tell me right now. I need to take them down before security finds them and you get in trouble."

Ha, wouldn't you like to know if you got them all?

"Are you trying to threaten me, Philip?" Sofie's voice was calm with a hint of ridicule. What kind of threat was that anyway? Getting in trouble with security. What was this? A shopping mall?

Philip took an auditable breath.

"I'm trying to help you."

"Of course you are."

"Look," he continued ignoring her sarcasm, "I don't know who you are, but I think you're in over your head. If I can get to you, then Security will too. And he doesn't issue threats first."

Philip used the word Security like a name. Like it was someone to be feared. Someone who could not be contained. Someone who was capable of doing unspeakable things to her once he found her.

"I appreciate the heads up, Philip."

She meant it. If Elandra was as dangerous as he claimed, he would be in trouble simply by telling her this. Unless, of course, he was the one in charge. In that case, he was trying to lower her defences by playing the protector.

"Why are you so glib?" Philip was getting annoyed and Sofie could hear him pace in his bedroom. "How do you know that Security isn't tracing you right now? Hm? Finding out where you live? Because I don't! He might be on his way to resolve this little issue?" Philip's voice had become louder. "He could already be at your door. Don't you understand? Breaking in while we argue. He could ..."

"Philip," Sofie interrupted his erratic spout of words. "I'm touched that you're worried about me. But there's no need."

She had to snicker at the thought of them actually trying to geo-trace her. Her mobile rerouted calls and she would show up in Tunisia or Korea right now. She had been in the business long enough to know the tricks and rules to survive. Like never to disclose her mobile number. In fact, her number was virtual and automatically changed everyday. Philip got lucky. Tumbling through the maze in the brief moment in time when everything was still aligned. Tomorrow it would reset and there was no way for him to reach her again without getting lost in dead ends and blind turns.

But he didn't know that; didn't need to know. He was a pawn in her game and it was time to make her move.

"You know what else touches me, Philip?" She said, not even hiding the satisfied grin in her voice. "You calling my name when you come."

Her offhand bawdy statement was met with silence. It was a low blow but she could not resist following the smell of blood in the water.

"I see." He took a deep breath. "I thought you were a professional. But you're not, are you? You are a reckless thrill seeker, not recognizing that a strategic retreat is your best option. That's too bad. I wonder what we could have achieved together with a more measured approach."

Bastard. His confidence was infuriating, it seemed nothing could faze him for long. Sofie could not help but set him straight.

"Measured approaches are for people who give up when things get too difficult. And by the looks of it that's exactly what you did tonight. After making such a big deal of not enjoying yourself you gave up the first chance you've got with Ms Hunt."

"You are jealous..."

Sofie could hear his smile. Instead of being embarrassed he was excited. Why? Was it because it gave him more leverage against or it meant something to him? In any case, Sofie reeled from how quickly the tables had turned against her. She was indeed jealous and him calling it out made it painfully obvious how much of an effect he had on her. She envied every single one of Philip's clients, who had the ability to summon him whenever they liked, while she had to resort to trickery to get his attention.

"But to answer your question..." He lowered his voice to a dangerous purr. "I broke my rules tonight because I was excited that our interactions weren't over. That you wanted to stay connected. Wanted to watch me. And knowing the effect it would have on you... It simply turned me on too much."

He cleared his throat and continued matter-of-factly, "tonight made me also realize how much this little wimp of mine interferes with my work. I cannot allow this to go on. We need to wrap up our engagement so both of us can get back to normal. So, Miss Carter, I can arrange one more visit. Free of charge, of course."

How cocky to even suggest that she was willing to entertain the idea of returning to their original deal after all her trickery. But she was even more furious about her wanting nothing more than to do exactly that. To be back in his suite; back in his arms, sampling all he had to offer. But it wasn't possible.

"I can't do that, Philip."

This was the first time he showed real vulnerability. And there was no way she wouldn't exploit that. Ruthless? Maybe, but for the greater good. MP Kerry was a big story but there were many more stories like this in Philip's treasure chest. All of them needed to be exposed. All of them Sofie wanted to have. And tonight he disclosed that there was a real chance for her to actually own them. That she had the power to make him give them up. Not for money or power but out of love.

"Can't or won't do that?"

A dangerous edge crept into his voice. Had he already caught on to her new plan?

"Sleeping with someone is a big deal for me," Sofie hedged. "I don't want to do it in a room where you had sex with hundreds of women before. I want to meet outside of Elandra? Have dinner? Take it from there?"

Getting him away from his home turf would be the first step to making him see her like a woman he could fall in love with, not a client he renders a service to.

"Are you asking me on a date?"

Sofie smiled. She savoured the thrill of asking the infamous Philip out on a date. Seducing him on her own terms. That was indeed a challenge worth accepting.

"Yes, I am."

"I don't date, Miss Carter. Least of all you."

His voice was curt. Too curt. He did not rebuff her because he wasn't interested. Far from it. She was actually getting somewhere!

"Why is that?"

"It's too dangerous."

"Oh c'mon. You're allowed to have a private life, aren't you? Where is the harm in having one dinner with me?"

There was a long silence on the line. He was struggling with his answer. Not so calm anymore, are you?

"I can't leave the compound."

"What do you mean? You'll be going to the city with Ms Hunt."

"That's a business trip. There'll be a driver. He'll be with me until I am back at Elandra."

He has a handler? The confident and enigmatic player was in fact a caged panther. All the elegance, wealth and power were his restraints. They were the bars that contained him and cut him off from the world.

"You are living in a cage, Philip!"

Was he lonely? Bored? Yearning to be free? He must be, how could he not?

"I don't see it that way. Yes, I have a demanding employer. Elandra requires dedicated commitment, it's not just a nine-to-five job. But I get paid accordingly and we are creating something truly unique. We are pioneering a service for women that has been available to men for millennia. No one has ever changed the paradigm or built an empire without some sacrifices. I get to create a legacy here."

"It might be a golden cage in a new kind of zoo. But it's still a cage. How can you not see that? You are their prisoner, Philip!"

"Hold on, I wouldn't go quite that far. I could leave if I wanted to, I just couldn't return."

"Why not?"

"Because, Miss Carter, what I do requires a high level of trust. My clients want provenance on everything I did and that's only possible if Elandra oversees my every move."

"How can you not have a problem with that?"

"It wasn't restrictive..."

"Until now?"

She didn't need to phrase it as a question, the way his voice was trailing off made it clear that this was the case. It came out as a question because she could not quite believe how different his reality was to how she pictured it to be. Was this conversation his first glimpse in a while on an open horizon with endless possibilities? Reminding him what liberty tastes like? And how it felt to be asked what he wanted, instead of what's best for Elandra?

"Yes... until now." Mischief suddenly entered his voice, "I tell you what, I'll send you some coordinates. Let's meet there. Tomorrow. 11pm."

"Coordinates?"

"Well, yes. I'm afraid it's not a restaurant. But at least it's outside Elandra. That's unfortunately all I can offer for now."

It sounded so genuine, so enthusiastic, so gleeful that Sofie could not help but be sucked in.

"That's ok. I'm looking forward to it."

"Great, see you tomorrow."

The line disconnected. This conversation ended very differently from how it started. Suddenly her objective wasn't to gain leverage or manipulate him to give up his information anymore. Instead, she wanted to know him, be his confidant, perhaps even help him escape. Maybe it was better to be loved than feared, after all.

The phone buzzed with a text message.

Unknown number:51.245410 -0.368096. It's a date.

Her heart leapt at the last sentence. It certainly felt like a date. She pulled up an online map and typed in the coordinates. They came up as a meadow a couple of kilometers away from Elandra. In the woods. Away from any streets or towns. They would be alone, in the middle of the night.

Oh no!

She was either going to meet the real Philip or get murdered in the process.

Was she really willing to risk that? For what? The chance of getting to know Philip?

Prepare for the worst

S ofie had been looking forward to her date with Phillip. But in the cold hard light of the day her 'date' looked more like a trap. She wanted to trust Philip. But was she naive for doing so? In unclear situations like these, Sofie resorted to collecting more intel. But there wasn't more to be found out about Philip. So instead she put her trust in technology, equipping herself with gadgets that could get her through any hairy situation she might encounter tonight.

The doorbell of the little hardware store played the theme song of X-file as Sofie entered. She found this place on the internet. It was on the outskirts of London and suitably small to not be asking uncomfortable questions or requiring identification. The only online review read 'dodgy and strange'. It was a great endorsement for a spy-store, especially one that could serve Sofie's unusual and borderline legal requirements.

An unpleasant mixture of mildew and soldering fumes hit her as she stepped over a mountain of old mail into the one-room shop. The place was stuffed to the ceiling with boxes containing radio-transmitters, surveillance cameras and computer chips. Looking around the windowless room, she noticed a half dead indoor plant in one corner and a life size mannequin with a baseball cap and bulletproof vest in the other.

An oversized glass vitrine took up most of the dingy room. It displayed the shop's more pricey items. Sofie recognised the CSR-PRO-3000, a counter surveillance receiver developed for the Israeli military to locate any types of bugs, video transmitters, and tape recorders. With this bad boy, Elandra would have had no problem spotting her remaining camera. Luckily, this device was not part of the standard equipment for security personnel, at least not in this country. Sofie didn't recognize any of the other devices in the display case. They presumably had similarly left-field application areas. Half of them even looked custom made, with wires and oddly shaped antennas sticking out of the open casings. 'Strange' wasn't even covering how this place looked.

"I'll be out in just a second..." a male voice called from the back room.

With a sudden loud bang, several cardboard boxes came tumbling through the curtain that separated the back from the shop's display area. The shop-keeper let out a pained groan.

"Are you ok?" Sofie tried to peek through the gap in the fabric but it was too dark to see.

"Fine, fine," the voice shouted. "Maybe like this... Um, no... Ah, darn. I'm stuck... They delivered the shipment to the wrong entrance, and now... Sorry, not your problem... Do you mind coming to the back? I cannot get out."

Sofie smiled, 'dodgy' was also a very accurate description. She carefully stepped over a wild tangle of power extensions and cables that crisscrossed the room to various monitors and machines. This place was a mess and a fire hazard on top of it. But given that nothing seemed to have exploded so far and the monitors weren't even flickering, the person running this place knew what they were doing. This certainly was the right place to upgrade her gear for tonight's assignment.

She pushed the blotchy green curtain to the side to find an elderly man surrounded by hundreds of little boxes containing GPS trackers. Clearing up this mess without crushing any of the fragile content would take a while. No wonder he summoned her to the back instead of trying to forge a path out of it.

"How can I help you, tod- ...," his milky-blue eyes landed on Sofie and he let out a loud sigh. "I don't have time for this today, dear. Tell Mike his jokes aren t funny anymore."

"I don't know any Mike," Sofie huffed. The old man's eyesight seemed to not be the best and he must have confused her with somebody else. "I need some Dal Model 2 motion sensors..."

"Yes yes, ...baked into a cheesecake, I suppose? Or installed inside a ship in a bottle? Look, you're obviously an actress, and I'm obviously busy. So let's skip to the part where you tell Mike that I'm now working on the ridiculously time consuming thing you supposedly commissioned. Yes?"

"What? Why would I be an actress?"

The old man studied her for a second, genuinely puzzled by her question.

"You are well dressed, attractive, and you know what you want."

"And that's unusual?"

"Yes. Dear. People who come here are... well... not normal."

"I see..." Sofie checked her watch. Only six hours left until showtime and there was so much more to do. "Just tell me where I can find the sensors and how much you want for 20 of them. Then you can go straight back to what you were doing."

"20? Are you sure? Dals are top of the range sensors. Wide angle, 30 meters range, night vision... What could you possibly need 20 of them for?"

This unusual request piqued the old man's interest. Sofie suddenly fitted in with his 'not normal' clientele.

"Surveillance."

"Yes, yes, but what area are we talking about here. A room? A courtyard?"

"A Meadow."

"Oh wow, ok."

There was excitement in his eyes. It was an interesting scenario and he enjoyed putting together the perfect solution. "How are you planning to connect them?"

Sofie was pleased that he didn't probe deeper about the reasons or specifics but instead talked shop about the technical details. This place was perfect.

"Wifi, with a booster every 50 meters."

"Sure. That could work. But I have something better... Let me show you."

He went down on his knees to gently coax the GPS-tracker boxes to the side. After several armfuls he had created a path for him to leave his paper prison. He got up and hobbled on unsteady legs out to the showroom, motioning for Sofie to follow him. He unlocked the vitrine with a key that was dangling on a chain from his khaki cord pants. It all felt very last century, which probably was when the heydays of his career were.

"There." He held up a device that wasn't much larger than a mobile phone. It had a thick antenna on one side and a screen on the other. "I made it last year, it connects to the Dal sensors and makes them talk to each other."

Sofie took the little machine, it was light and portable. The old man hooked both his thumbs under the pair of suspenders that held the pants over his round belly and rocked back and forth on his heels. He was proud of his invention.

"You can triangulate the object moving through the sensor net. Estimate the size and speed. I even have a little experimental AI running that judges properties. like if someone is crouching or walking."

"This is perfect!" Sofie was impressed. The machine even looked more put together than the other prototypes. "Are you sure it works with 20 Dals though?"

"Never tested that. But I can't see a reason it wouldn't. Let's set it up and try."

The excitement in the old man's face was heart-warming. He was a true inventor. Building devices just because they were technologically possible. So coming across a use case that needed the features of his creation must be the best validation for his genius he could ask for.

But this man was more than just a genius inventor. There was a wistfulness in him that came from years of experience in the field.

"This is not just surveillance, dear. Is it? You are expecting hostiles."

The old man studied Sofie, as she counted out the 20 Dals for the test and debated with herself how much of her mission she wanted to share with him.

"Why do you ask?"

"I understand that you don't want to share details. I don't mean to pry. But I think you should get protective equipment as well." He nodded over to the mannequin with the bulletproof vest.

Sofie shook her head, "Yeah, that's not an option, I'm afraid."

She had to chuckle at the thought of Philip undressing her only to find her wearing Kevlar-laced underwear instead of tempting lingerie.

"At least..." The old man hesitated but decided to go ahead with his statement after all. "Get something for self-defence."

He propped open a hidden compartment underneath the glass vitrine. He opened it just a crack, only enough for Sofie to see tasers, pepper sprays and ear-poppers. All of this was illegal in the UK, no wonder he hesitated to show her. God knows what else was hidden in that drawer. What kind of damsel in distress did he think she was? Or did he put her into the hot-headed thrill seeker category, like Philip? Either way, this wasn't her style.

"I don't think I'll be needing this."

"Think or know?"

The concern in his voice made Sofie consider his question.

"I don't know, but I also don't plan to stay around if things go pear shaped."

"Not everything can be controlled, child. But what you can always do is prepare for the worst."

His droopy blue eyes held hers. They had a sad intensity to them that spoke of lived experience. It reminded Sofie of her father. He would have been his age now. Sofie suddenly felt the overwhelming urge to hug him and tell him that everything would be fine, just like she did twenty years ago in the hospital, when her father's scarred lungs wouldn't fill with air anymore. Her father had been a construction worker and years of asbestos exposure made his lungs give out when he was just 53.

His disease progressed so fast that there was little time to say goodbye, let alone get justice for what the company did to him. They knew that the material they used was contaminated, yet they never protected him or any of the other workers. But no one took them to court. Why would I want to spend my last days being angry? That's what he had said. But Sofie knew that the real reason for him not seeking justice was because he didn't think he could win. And he was probably right.

After his death Sofie felt helpless and alone, just a pawn in an unjust world. That's when she vowed to never feel vulnerable like this ever again. To never back down from a fight and to bring justice to those who could not take it for themselves.

She looked at the old shopkeeper, wondering what wrong he had to endure. Who he had lost to become so weary. A wife, a daughter perhaps?

Maybe he was right? Breaking the law suddenly did not feel like such a deterrent. If it gave her the chance to protect herself and fight her fight for longer, why not take it.

"Ok fine, I might get the taser."

A relieved smile whisked over the old man's face, like he had managed to save her from a preventable evil, just like someone should have saved his loved one in the past. He handed her the taser. It felt heavy, cold and foreign. She instinctively knew that if she had to use this weapon she would be fighting for her life. It drove home how dangerous tonight could get.

Sofie left the shop an hour later, after they tested the sensor net and confirmed that everything was working as intended. But the old man's words and the weight of the taser stuck with her on the drive home. You can always prepare for the worst. She certainly was physically prepared. No one would move in that meadow without her knowing and the taser would take care of the rest. But was she mentally prepared? How would she feel if Philip turned on her? If he revealed that he was the head of Elandra and had been working with MP Kerry just like her sources claimed? That the first person she'd wanted to trust in years was a criminal.

There was only one way to find out!

Your plaything

Philip's rendezvous point was in the middle of the forest. It was dark, secluded and the very place that screamed "danger". Sofie had been here since before sunset to prepare the sensor net. Back then, it was beautiful, with birds chirping and butterflies playing in the mild afternoon breeze. Maybe that's the image Philip had in mind when he suggested this place, at least that's what she hoped.

But Sofie was prepared either way. Dozens of high-tech motion sensors lined the meadow, alerting her of anything moving in the undergrowth. She would not be ambushed. No one but Philip, would come close enough to hurt her And the old man's taser would take care of him trying anything.

The only thing left to do was disguise all of her preparations and make it look like she was here for a date. She set up the blanket, unwrapped the cheese platter and propped herself down, pretending to look out for Philip.

The lanterns around the blanket cast a soft light across the wildflower meadow. Leaning back, Sofie let her fingers rake through the lush earthy grass and inhaled the faint aromas from the surrounding pine trees. With all the risks mitigated, this actually was a beautiful place. The mist from the nearby stream made the air taste like rain and the soft hoot from owls felt like freedom. It cast her back to when she was a teenager, disobedient and wild, without a care in the world, waiting for the sweetheart of her mid-summer romance.

Fireflies danced over the stream when the perimeter alarm buzzed in her pocket. Someone was approaching. And not from the direction Elandra was located. Where Philip should have come from. Sofie's heart rate quickened. She wasn't waiting for her sweetheart, was she? She was waiting for a man she barely knew. And by the looks of it, he had even sent someone else. A henchman to abduct her. Or worse, finish her off right here. It surely was the place for it. Had she been reckless?

I'm not planning on sticking around if it goes pear-shaped. That's what she said to the old man, but it wasn't quite as clear cut now. The display showed a single person approaching, likely a man, walking leisurely towards the meadow. He wasn't running or sneaking, he wasn't trying to catch her by surprise. It could very well be Philip walking to his date, simply having taken a detour to savour his night of freedom. With a quick check on the taser, Sofie decided to wait for the man to arrive.

She breathed a sigh of relief, when it was indeed Philip who stepped out from the tree line into the moon-bathed meadow. The silver light twinkled over his easy smile and made Sofie's heart skip a beat. He was even more gorgeous than usual, wearing a black shirt and beige shorts. With a fire kindling in her heart, she watched him approach. Then she remembered her plan.

"Stop right there," she issued. "And take off your clothes."

Philip's eyebrow lifted in surprise and his smile faded. He'd expected a greeting and gotten a command instead that sounded unexpected and harsh even to her. This wasn't how he thought their night would begin.

"After what you've said on the phone," she tried to clarify, "you can't blame me for being cautious. I just want to make sure you're not armed..." She cleared her throat adding, "you can keep your underpants on."

"As you wish."

It sounded neutral. He was used to blunt commands like this... from being an escort? Or a criminal?

"Now, turn. Let me see your back. Show you're not hiding anything."

"Satisfied?"

He raised his arms to the side, biceps flexing and pecks tough, turning for her.

"Almost," she replied milder, trying to make up for the rocky start, "just leave your clothes there please and come over?"

With every step Philip managed to restore his smile, though the easiness that was there earlier never returned.

"Wine?"

"Yes." His eyes flicked over the wooden board with grapes, Camembert, Cheddar and crackers. "I see you didn't bring knives either. Not risking getting stabbed over being civilized, are you?"

"C'mon, don't be like that. Besides," she gave him a little wink, "I didn't think you were a stickler for conventions."

"What if I was?" he smiled. "Especially, with you breaking another convention. One that's even worse than butchering cheese."

"Oh yes? What's that?"

"Being fully dressed..." He popped a grape into his mouth. "While I'm half naked."

"Are you worried that I brought a weapon?"

"I'm not worried." He laughed, relaxing back onto his elbow. He looked like a roman statue: the male ideal, immortalized during an extravagant feast. "I know you brought one. It's hidden in your basket. A pocket knife, right? -- No wait," he gave her a mock disapproving look. "A taser."

Sofie's face fell, how could he know?

"You checked on it just before I came," he replied to her unspoken question. "It's something suitably small to fit in the basket, yet you were hesitant to touch it. So it's forbidden, like an illegal weapon. But you were too casual for it to be a deadly firearm. Other than that the taser was just a wild guess." He grinned. "I have another guess for you, Miss Carter: you've set up a perimeter alarm."

"That's ridiculous," Sofie snorted.

There was no way he could know that. And she wasn't going to confirm how tech-literate she was to someone just fishing for answers.

He crooked his head. "I didn't take the direct route from Elandra. Yet, you knew exactly where I was coming from."

"I heard something in the woods, so I turned to look."

"Nice try, but the stream is too noisy to hear anything approaching."

He set her up. He trusted her as little as she was trusting him. At least they were on the same page.

"I'm rather impressed, Miss Carter." He fixed her with an evaluating stare. "I've underestimated you. What are you? A police officer? Private investigator?"

Sofie's nerves tingled. Her plan to make him fall in love with her would have never worked. He was too careful, too suspicious. And on top of that, he was now getting dangerously close to the truth. Time to make a choice: give up on the YubiKey or give in to his deal.

"You can keep guessing," she replied with her mind made up, "or I can take off my dress... Your call."

He swallowed. The sudden turn took him by surprise and there was a struggle in his hooded eyes. Should he continue gathering intel or seize the moment? Mind over body?

"Ok, you win." He raked a hand through his brown hair. "Take off your clothes."

Body over Mind! At least this is going exactly as planned.

Sofie perched on her knees to slide down the front-zipper of her white sundress. The soft fabric fell to the side, revealing her lace bra and panties. Sitting back on her haunches, she slightly parted her legs; just enough to make Philip's eyes gravitate down. Temptation had engulfed him. Good.

"You're so beautiful, Sofie," he breathed, more to himself than her.

Hearing him say her name for the first time and in unhinged desire broke the dam that was so far successfully holding back her own lust. On her hands and knees she slowly crawled over, approaching him like a lioness, claiming her kill. He did not object when she set his wine glass aside. Nor did he try to hide his readiness, bulging between her legs as she straddled him. He wanted her.

Sofie could not resist grinding against him, watching mesmerized as he closed his eyes to savour the feeling. Yes, she too wanted him. But she wasn't here to enjoy herself. She was on a mission. Never forget that.

"So," she cooed. "Are we finalizing our transaction today, Philip?"

His hands moved up her thighs and cupped her buttock, sinking into her firm curves. He was lost in a different world. Orbiting around her.

"You can have whatever you want, Sofie." He breathed against her lips as his desperate kiss plundered her mouth.

He wasn't the controlled and deliberate lover from Elandra anymore. There was a primal yearning in his touch that carried her with him, like a raging river. She reached down inside his pants and his unrestrained response shifted something inside of her. It cut off the last anchor points to her mission. And without the weight of her ulterior motif, all the emotion that had built up since their first kiss flooded into her. With an unfamiliar urgency she freed him from the remaining piece of fabric, needing to feel the direct connection.

"Hold on," he rasped, "I need to... the condom... in my pants."

Seeing the devastating effect she had on the otherwise eloquent and con-trolled womanizer, turned the air around Sofie into fire. She needed to have him.

"I have one," she replied, ignoring his look of surprised victory. He hadn't expected her to plan for this outcome.

She hastily ripped the foil pack and unrolled it on his length. She let her head fall back in a moan as she made him plunge into her, drinking in the sweet ache from his size impaling her.

He groaned. His hands grabbed her hip to stop her from moving. He was already fighting to hold himself in check. Sofie bit back another moan. Seeing him get undone so quickly was damn hot.

When he opened his eyes again his brown iris glowed amber in the moonlight. He managed to only take off the edge from his desire for her.

"Slow down," he growled, when she steadily increased the speed. "I'm not used to this."

"Used to what?"

"Wanting someone..."

His confession made her only want to thrust harder; without finesse or technique. It was like serving a home cooked meal to a gourmet chef. He clearly disapproved. But the carnal hunger made it impossible for him to stop. There was something oh so sinful about devouring her offering.

He tried to guide her movements, but Sofie defied. She loved playing his body against his mind. And pushing him over the edge, gave her the salacious satisfaction she was craving.

Deep vibrations came from his chest as his release reverberated through his body. He never looked more beautiful than in this moment. And she never wanted him more.

"That was very wicked of you," he smiled as his breathing calmed. "Let me repay the favor."

He gently brushed her hair from her neck and trailed it with kisses. Her painfully unsatisfied body responded instantly, clenching around him and demanding more.

"Stop!" she bit out. The deed was done. That's all this was. Time to get what she came for. "Give me the YubiKey. Now!"

The amber glow left his eyes and a pained expression distorted his face as he scrambled out from underneath her. "I don't have it."

"What do you mean 'you don't have it'?" Sofie's breath caught in her lungs. "I've done everything you wanted. I've earned it."

Silence fell between them as Philip turned to fetch his clothes.

"You didn't bring the YubiKey!" she gasped, "You planned to deceive me! Didn't you?"

The realization hit her like a brick wall. He never meant to hand over the YubiKey. It was all just a game to him. A pastime, to see how far he could go with her. And she let him go all the way.

"That's not true!" He wheeled around, anger flashing in his eyes. "I didn't plan any of this. I didn't plan to risk my job to see you. Or losing control with you, like a teenage boy. And definitely, I didn't plan on being asked for payment. Not while I'm still inside you, for goodness sake."

He held up a hand to silence her reply. He needed a moment to regroup. "You really are something," he mumbled, while rubbing his forehead and taking a deep breath.

"The deal we agreed, Miss Carter, was to have sex in my suite. Like a regular client."

"Why does it matter where or how we do it?" She was angry about him dictating the terms and changing the rules. But most of all about him still seeing her as a regular client. "I know why you do this, Philip. You want to string me along. Your golden cage is boring, isn't it? And you crave distraction. Well that's too bad because I refuse to be your plaything!"

"This is not a game!"

Damn well it isn't. His information on MP Kerry, Ms Hunt and god knows how many other corrupt players needed to be exposed. The sooner the better.

"Then, why do you act like it is?"

"Don't pretend you're playing fair. You have an agenda, Miss Carter, and it goes far beyond the YubiKey."

Oh I see! Was that it? Was he really fishing for confirmation that it wouldn't be over after he handed over the YubiKey?

"Mmh, let's see. You only asked Ms Hunt about the royal commission, after you knew I was listening. You wanted me to hear another secret. Wanted to get me hooked."

"What can I say? I like to show off my collection," he said with an odd smile. "But it doesn't mean, Miss Carter, that you get to take everything you see. I decide when and where to give you my secrets. The sooner you accept that, the sooner I can actually hand over the evidence."

Despite the cool night air, Sofie felt her temperature spike. He didn't want to expose corruption for the greater good. He wanted to control when and how the players would be taken down. He was the puppet master. And he wanted her to become one of his puppets.

The harsh vibration from Sofie's proximity alert suddenly went off.

"Someone's coming!"

There was panic in Philip's eyes as he pulled her down to crouch next to him.

"Security is coming," he whispered.

He is mine

The perimeter alarm cut through Sofie and Philip's heated argument, like a leopard breaking apart the dominance fight of two antelopes. "Security" was coming and Philip was on high alert. Was he afraid for his or her safety? Or was this one of his carefully planned ploys?

"How much time do we have?" Philip's voice was a low growl as his eyes darted along the tree line.

Sofie's perimeter monitor calculated the speed and distance of the approaching person. "About two minutes." It judged the person to be male and at a walking pace. "Why are you so concerned?"

"I told you Security is dangerous. If Elandra suspects I'm gone..." He closed his eyes for a second to collect his thoughts. "Let's not get into this. Help me clean this up."

He hastily stuffed the half-eaten cheese platter into the basket and pushed the blanket on top, gesturing for Sofie to collect the lanterns.

"Hurry up!" His tone was sharp. "Where is he coming from?"

"From over there." Sofie pointed towards the forest path, leading to one of Elandra's fences. "I don't understand, why is..."

"And this is not the time to explain," he grabbed her arm to make her look at him, "I'll distract him so you can get away. Your car is nearby, yes?"

"Yes, but it's right where he's coming from. He could have seen it."

"Damit!"

Philip raked both hands through his hair and started pacing.

Seeing Philip lose his cool made cold shivers run up her spine. She was in danger.

"Is the car traceable to you?"

"No."

It was a rental. She got it under a false ID and paid in cash.

"Ditch it and get a ride from the highway."

"Are you serious? I can't get a cab out here, I'd have to hitchhike..."

How could he even suggest that?

"Trust me, it's safer than running into him. You still have your taser, right?"

Sofie grabbed his arm, the seriousness of the situation had sunken in.

"Philip, will you be alright?"

When he did not reply she added, "come with me. Away from all of this... I know I haven't been open with you, but..."

"Sofie..." He sounded calmer. "I can't come with you. And you must go now. Please."

There was nothing else to say. He made up his mind and there wasn't enough time for Sofie to change it. With a curt nod, she stepped into the woods. The dense forest wrapped itself around her like a blanket of shadows, hiding her from the brightly lit meadow. But the thick underwood caught in her hair and tore at her clothes. With every step twigs snapped and leaves rattled. This is too noisy. She glanced back at Philip. He shook his head.

"Stay hidden," he mouthed and returned to the middle of the meadow.

"There you are!"

A man dressed in a black combat uniform stepped onto the meadow. His clenched jaw made his angular face hollow and corded. His nose looked like it had been broken several times and never quite healed. This was a man who lived and breathed physical conflict.

Without hesitation he drew his gun and pointed it at Philip. Sofie pressed her hand over her mouth to silence a gasp. This must be Security. How could he treat one of their own like that?

"Why are you pointing your gun at me, Security?" Phillip asked with surprising casualty.

"Because I won't have any of your fucking mindgames, Primo."

Despite his crude and intimidating behaviour, Security's body was tense. He was uncomfortable with Philip. "I won't end like Yates. He is still in the loony bin."

"Yates was ill. Him losing it has nothing to do with me. You know that." Philip smirked. "And if it did, a gun wouldn't help you. So, put it away."

"Just shut your mouth and put your hands behind your head."

Security lifted his wrist to speak into his radio.

"I got Primo. He is in Delta 3. Eagle1, search the area. Over."

"That's not necessary. I was just going for a walk."

"At night?"

"Yes. Your rules, remember? I can't be near the fences by day in case people see me." Philip scratched the back of his head, "Look, I needed to get out. Take a proper hike, you know? Not just the 15 min from one fence to the other. It was foolish of me, Brent. Ok? I'm sorry. Let's get back to Elandra and grab a beer together. Yeah?"

Brent's expressions softened. He searched Philip's face for the truth. "Yeah, all right. You're buying, and I wanna hear how you did the Indian chick."

Philip's magic knew no boundaries. We're all just people in the end. Except for Philip. He was a chameleon, able to perfectly adjust to the situation at hand. Giving everyone what they wanted or at least pretending to.

Brent lowered his gun, when the radio suddenly croaked.

"Security? We found a car. Engine's cold. It's been here for a couple of hours. Over."

"You rat!" Brent spat, pointing his gun back at Philip. "Who'd you meet?"

"No one." Philip's brows furrowed, like this was a far-fetched idea. "How would I even talk to anyone outside? You monitor my calls."

Security flashed him a toothy grin. He was not going to buy his lies a second time.

"Eagle1, Eagle2. I want the woods around the meadow searched. Thoroughly. Over."

"That's really not necessary, the car could..."

"I say what's necessary," Brent shouted.

"C'mon Brent. I wouldn't..."

"I had it with you and your manipulations. You'll show respect and address me with the proper honorifics."

Security's veins throbbed in his forehead and with the back of his gloved hand he slapped Philip across the face. Sofie clenched her teeth at the loud smack of leather hitting skin. Philip's head snapped to the side. A dark cloud rolled over his eyes as he wiped his lip.

"Need I remind you, Security," Philip said holding up his bloodied hand, "that Elandra will not take it lightly if you make me unfit for work."

"You think you are such a hotshot, aren't you?" Security's nostrils flared. "The notorious Philip. The star of Elandra. Well guess what, Primo, Elandra ordered to terminate you. That's how much Elandra values you."

The color drained from Philip's face.

"That's ridiculous. I was gone for less than 3 hours."

"Elandra's top asset went AWOL. Every minute counts to minimize damage," Security explained as if talking to a disobedient schoolboy. "And you walking around like that? It's a big liability. Eladra won't risk that for long."

Security stepped closer. He was half a head taller than Philip and his bulk towered over him.

"Why the trollops tell you all their secrets is beyond me." He trailed the barrel of his gun along Philip's cheek, as if to caress him. "Especially, since they all regret it afterwards. They all call the next day. In a panic. Pleading to sort it out. Sort you out." Security grabbed Philip's chin and tapped the gun against Philip's cheek with every word. "Yet. They. Keep. Feeding. You. Filling that pretty little head of yours with information. So stupid. So dangerous for you."

"I signed a non-disclosure agreement. You know I'm no risk."

Security laughed menacingly. He was in control and he enjoyed it.

"Oh? I can think of ways to make you talk. No contract in the world would have kept you silent once I was through with you. And I'm sure others could do too."

He let the cruelty of his statement sink in.

"You look shocked, Primo." Security's voice turned to a dangerous rumble, "You probably don't know how whores are treated in the real world."

He pressed the gun against Philips' forehead.

"I think I'll show you. Right now." A sleazy snarl curved his lips. "On your knees, Primo."

"You're not afraid of my mind tricks anymore?" asked Philip meekly as he sank to his knees in front of Security.

"No I'm not," he laughed. "You won't be able to talk when you choke on my dick!"

Sofie reeled at the guard's crude language and callus demeanor. She needed to do something to save Philip from this brute, but her taser wouldn't work through all that combat armor. She could only watch in horror as Security unzipped his fly and dug one-handedly into his pants. He was standing with his back to Sofie, She couldn't see what's going on, but judging from Philip's dismayed expression, Security must have readied himself. Sofie's stomach flipped.

Security grabbed a handful of Philip's brown hair and forced his face closer.

"And the squat?" Philip gasped. "What if they find us? They are still searching the woods."

Security stopped his assault and fumbled for the radio.

"Eagle1, Eagle2." His voice sounded breathless. "Stand down. Return to base. Confirm. Over."

The radio stayed silent for a second.

"Security? Everything ok, Boss? Over."

"Eagle1, follow your damn orders. Over and Out."

Security switched off the radio.

"There. No one will interrupt us." The guard licked his lips in anticipation. "Now, open your mouth for me."

"Careful, Brent." Philip's voice changed. There was an authority in it that no man on his knees should have. "You might be able to do this to me out here. But back at Elandra, I am out of your reach. I'm the Primo. You'll see me everyday. Think about how good my mouth felt on you. Never to have it again. Is that what you want? Have your mind poisoned like that?" He paused before adding, "What do you think this did to Yates? Drive him crazy?"

A yelp emanated from the Security's throat. His eyes protruded and his jaw muscles pulsed as he contemplated the implications.

"You think you'll get out of it just like that? Elandra authorized the kill. I can have my fun and then..." Security mimicked the recoil of his gun.

"The others know you found me, Brent. What do you think Elandra will do to you if you kill me for no reason? You're just the muscle, easily replaceable, compared to the one who brings in the money." Philip got up from his knees. "We are done here."

"I don't think so?" Security, hissed through his teeth, before slamming the handle of his gun into Philip's face. A sickening crack echoed down the meadow as blood gushed from Philip's nose.

"There, that'll teach ya." Security added another punch that sent Philip to the ground. "Now, we're done."

A half-smile crept into Philip's face as he groggily collected himself up again.

"What are you smiling about? No one's gonna fuck you looking like that."

"True, my calendar will be wide open." Philip laughed as his eyes trailed over the tree line where Sofie was standing.

"With that attitude you won't stay Primo for long." Rage made Brent's voice vibrate. "And when Elandra's done with you, I'll be there. Waiting. Ready." He grabbed his groin and fletched his teeth in a desperate attempt to match Philip's confidence.

"Until then, Brent. Walk me back, will you?"

Sofie exhaled as the two men disappeared into the forest. Philip had indeed been risking a lot to see her tonight, and even more to protect her. To get her out he had to play with fire. Take calculated risks to manipulate the guards. Making them call off the search. He expertly bent Security to his will. That was skill, even if he had to take a beating for it. For her. Or was that the outcome he wanted to achieve? Clearing his calendar? After all, she heard his invitation loud and clear.

But I'm not doing that. Philip could not always get what he wanted. Instead, she was going to create a plan to get him out of there. Elandra was toxic and potentially deadly. He needed to leave, whether he could see it or not. And his London date with Ms Hunt was the perfect escape route.

'He is mine.' That's what she would say to Ms Hunt. And Sofie couldn't wait to see Philip's face, when she did.

Know the enemy

W as it bold or downright delusional to think Sofie could snatch Philip away from Ms. Hunt? Unlike Sofie, Ms. Hunt was an exotic beauty, fabulously rich, and used to getting what she wanted. She wouldn't give up a date just because Sofie asked her to. Neither would Philip. He'd see the evening through, out of loyalty or fear. So if she had any chance of luring him away, she needed time alone with him to convince him that leaving Elandra was the right choice. For that, she had to come up with a plan that made Ms. Hunt want to leave but not before Philip was safely out of Elanra's clutches.

To come up with this perfect plan she needed to know the enemy. She spent the past week observing Ms. Hunt. Like Philip, the woman was absolutely dedicated to her work. Maybe that's what they bonded over? She left for the office at 5 in the morning and seldom came home before 8 at night. She ate at the office, had her deliveries sent there and even received her personal trainer and beautician there. Good. This made it easier to come up with a believable emergency, because there was only one address she could be called to: the office.

Sofie's basic plan was simple. It would have to do with the Royal Commission. If they found her skeletons, things could go pear shaped quickly and a late night emergency sitting of the executive team was plausible. So all she had to do was fill in the details. Who else would be at this meeting? What would convince Ms. Hunt to come? And how would she get there? All of this information could be found inside Ms. Hunt's headquarters. But that was easier said than done. Sofie wasted two days, trying to secure a fake badge, before giving up. It was her last day and she had to resort to trickery to get in.

"Shoot, I almost forgot you..." Sofie wheeze, jogging back to the reception desk.

She pretended to have come from the elevators of Ms. Hunt's insurance company and be on her way out of the building. This place was built to impress, taking up the entire footprint of the high-rise building and sporting a ten-meter high sculpture in the middle. During rush hour, it was bursting with the thousands of employees working here, but at three in the afternoon, only the 10 people operating the reception and check-in gates were around.

"What can I get you?" Sofie's overly excited voice echoed from the marble cladding as she called out to the lobby staff.

"What?"

One of the security guards looked up from his newspaper. He had a tired, resigned look on his face, like he was done with the day already.

"I didn't bring a birthday cake this year," she said as if that explained anything. "Evil carbs, and all... Instead, I'm getting everyone a COFFEE."

Sofie smiled stupidly as if this was the brightest idea she'd had all year.

"What are you on about?"

His tone turned hostile, the last thing he needed today was an enthusiastic moron to deal with.

"It's all in the email..." A quick glance at his name tag and jam-smeared shirt armed Sofie with enough information to start her scam. "Didn't you get it, Larry? Oh, by the way, how are the kids? You still have to do the school-runs?"

"Um, yes... How'd you know?"

His sleep deprived brain wasn't catching up, instead it told him to feel guilty for having forgotten who she was. He helplessly looked to another guard but that person just shrugged, his job was to sign-in people not bond with them.

"I'm the same, remember? But I dropped to part-time a while back. Now, I'm only in on Mondays. Makes it so much..."

"Happy Birthday." A guy with a nervous twitch under his left eye interrupted their conversation lacklustre. "I'll have an Americano."

It wasn't clear whether he believed her or just wanted his next caffeine fix. Either way, Sofie was grateful, because it opened the floodgates for the others to shout out their own coffee orders.

"Hang on," Sofie pointed to the fourth receptionist, "did you want a Latte or Cappuccino? You know what, can you write it down?"

Perfect. This would be her ticket back in. With an arm-full of coffee, they wouldn't try to scan her batch and buzz her straight through.

With the list in hand, Sofie headed for the little coffee place around the corner. She pushed open the door at the same time as a woman in her late thirties rushed out. Inevitably they collided, sending Sofie's valuable list to the ground along with the women's phone and lunch order.

"Watch where you're going, dumb bitch," the women hissed, boring her ice blue eyes through Sofie. She flicked her perfectly curled blond hair over her shoulder and tried to bend down to pick up the dropped items. Her tight skirt and four inch heels made the process harder than it should have been. It was like watching a frozen tree sway and creek in the arctic winds, except this ice queen chose her predicament by donning this impractical outfit. After a couple of failed attempts she gave up and snapped at Sofie.

"You mind?"

Sofie sighed and collected the paper bag for her. The woman's phone was still unlocked when Sofie reached for it. It showed a half written message to Boris Kluger saying 'Photo-ops w/ Ms Hunt 2mr @ Ba-'.

Photo opportunity with Ms. Hunt tomorrow at...

She didn't finish the name of the place. Why was the Ice Queen emailing a paparazzo? He usually snapped B-list celebrities for tabloids, not business women. Was she earning a quick buck on the site, leaking information about Ms. Hunt's diary? If so, where would she get that information from? Unless... Sofie smiled, this was better than getting inside the headquarters, this was like tapping straight into Ms. Hunt's brain.

"You are Ms. Hunt's secretary," Sofie announced, pretending to just recognize her.

"Personal assistant," the woman corrected while looking in disgust at the picked-up napkins Sofie was handing her.

"I'm so glad I ran into you. I'm new and Ms. Hunt asked me to call her driver. But I screwed up and forgot his name, can you..."

"No," the Ice Queen interrupted, looking at her like she was a rodent about to be devoured. "I arrange her travel."

"Then you can give me his number," Sofie pressed on, ignoring the crawling feeling you get when realizing you are talking to a psychopath.

"N.O."

Without another word, the Ice Queen rushed out of the shop. She didn't expect Sofie to follow, no one in their right mind would push their luck further after this exchange. They were half-way down the block when the Ice Queen noticed her tail. "I said 'No', are you deaf?"

"Don't be like that. I need your help. I don't wanna screw up the first thing I've been asked to do."

"Newsflash, mousy: incompetent people won't make it here."

"You are a backstabbing bitch," Sofie muttered, "and I thought you were just distracted by this thing tomorrow when she introduced me."

It was a gamble and could very well backfire. But this psychopath was her best chance of getting all the information she needed. She just had to poke her where it hurts. And if the messages she sent to Boris was about Ms. Hunt's date with Philip tomorrow, she had a good chance of finding a sore spot, because she had inside information.

The Ice Queen stopped in her tracks and wheeled around.

"Who said that? And how'd you know about the dinner?"

"I'm his cousin," Sofie shrugged, going all in with her bluff.

The Ice Queen's cold eyes evaluated her. Had she extended herself too much? Was this too far-fetched? Was it all coming crashing down?

"Proof it."

OK. She was at least buying that there could be nepotism in Ms. Hunt's company. This gave Sofie a bit more rope to carefully apply pressure; see if something cracks.

"I don't need to... I'll just tell Ms. Hunt that she's right about you. See, how long you keep your job."

"Good luck with that," the Ice Queen laughed. "If anything, I'd get a pay rise for weeding out dimwits."

Dammit! Wrong move. She probably should have known: It takes another psychopath to tolerate one as her personal assistant. Sofie needed to think fast, if there was any chance to turn this around. And the only way to 'proof it' would be to know where they were going.

Unfortunately, Sofie had no clue. All she knew was that it was a hyped up new restaurant in West End. Her research had narrowed it down to five options. And she'd been so sure that it was a toss-up between Calbresi and The Flame House, that she didn't look carefully at the other options. But since the restaurant had to start with "Ba" both choices seemed to be wrong. With the Ice Queen's unnerving eyes on her, Sofie racked her brain for the other two names, and whether one of them was actually starting with "Ba".

"It's Bamborino," Sofie said with all the confidence she could muster.

Ice Queen's face froze.

"You've seen it on my phone."

"Check it."

This time Sofie did not have to fake confidence. She watched as the Ice Queen realized that she never wrote the full name and how slim the odds were of picking the right name out of thin air. The wheels in her brain visibly turned as she calculated how to best exploit her opportunity to help a family member of Ms. Hunt's lover.

"Let's start over, shall we?" she canted, like the psychopath she was. "I'm Jennifer. You wanted her driver's name right? It's Jerome and this is his number." She held up her phone.

"Hey," she casually added while Sofie was copying down the number, "do you know what's it about?"

"What's what about?"

"Ms. Hunt asked me to slip the paparazzi where she'd be tomorrow. She's planning to announce something. Do you know what?"

Oh, so she didn't leak the info, Ms. Hunt directed her to. Interesting! What was the other psychopath playing at?

"Yes," Sofie lied, wondering if the curious secretary would leak more information.

"And...? Oh I see. You don't have to tell me, just say 'yes' or 'no': Does it have to do with MP Kerry?"

"Yes."

Sofie had no idea what the connection could be but getting more information about Kerry was a bonus.

"I knew it," Jennifer smiled. "Kerry's office gave us a courtesy call yesterday." Her air-quotes around 'courtesy' let slip what she really thought about their intentions.

"I heard," Sofie pretended. "They just wanted to scare us, right?"

"That's what I said! But it totally worked on Mr. Ibuvio. He ran around like a headless chicken all day."

"Who's Mr. Ibuvio again?"

"Hello? Head of public relations?" Jennifer mocked. "You aren't the brightest, are you? Where did they slot you in?"

"Finance."

"Of course."

"What?"

"Oh, c'mon. Nepotism department, much? Everybody knows that the chief financial officer is Hunt's mother." Jennifer rolled her eyes. "Just because she calls herself Mrs. Khan now doesn't fool anybody. Hunt was her first husband."

So hiring family was actually a thing. No wonder Jennifer believed her on the spot.

"Well," Sofie faked offence, "but I'm not family."

"Didn't you say you're the cousin of that finance guy she's going out with? She's quite cagey about him so I guess it's pretty serious between them."

Obviously not, if she's having her pictures taken with Philip tomorrow. Poor guy, he's probably getting dumped instead of proposed to. Although she might come back to him after Philip vanishes from Elandra.

With satisfaction Sofie went through the checklist in her head. She had more than enough to beef up her plan and make it believable. She glanced at her watch.

"Gotta go."

She left the Ice Queen standing like she had done the other way around just moments earlier.

It was time to get back home. Time to log into Philip's camera, just like she had done twice a day for the past week. But tonight was special, even though he did not know it yet. Tonight would be his last night at Elandra, and Sofie wanted to commemorate that on his behalf.

I need to talk to you

S ofie connected to the camera in Philip's room. Like the other times, the door to his room stayed closed. No wonder. Security's beating caused cuts and bruises that broke the illusion of him being Prince Charming. It ripped him straight out of their fantasy world and made him human to his clients. It wasn't a good look and bad for business.

While this deterred his clients, it felt different to Sofie. He took that beating for her. He protected her. For all intents and purposes, he was her Prince Charming. Sofie wasn't going to share him with anyone, least of all with Ms. Hunt. So knowing that no one else had been with him since their night in the woods gave her a domineering satisfaction.

She was about to log off when Philip stepped into the frame. His injuries had faded. Only a light pink hue on his cheek and nose remained from his daring stunt. Despite this, he didn't look like someone who enjoyed a week off work. He had dark rings under his eyes and a haunted expression on his face. Something was keeping him up at night. Not surprising, anyone finding out that their employer sent an assassin to terminate them, would look a bit green around the gills.

He leaned his back against the wall and looked into the camera.

"Why are you doing this to me?" he asked quietly.

The bitterness in his voice made Sofie's blood run cold. He found the last camera and was talking to her. Why are you doing this to me? What could he possibly mean by that? They hadn't spoken in a week. Whatever it was wasn't important right now. There was something bigger at stake. If he destroyed this camera just like he did with the first one, he would kill her only link into his world. She would be flying blind for her mission tomorrow. Jennifer gave her the name of the restaurant but she didn't know what time they would meet. If she missed him, he'd be trapped at Elandra, out of reach and locked in his golden cage forever. She took a deep breath to slow her racing thoughts.

"I know you've been watching," he sighed. It wasn't an accusation, he simply stated the facts. "You've logged into the camera for the last week. You log in, stay for half an hour and then you're gone."

He dropped his eyes to the floor, before looking straight at the camera again. His gaze met hers, bridging the digital void between them.

"Why are you watching me, instead of coming here?"

His sadness sent an arrow to her core.

She had wanted to come, rescue him, take him to safety. But Elandra was a formidable foe and underestimating them could have fatal consequences. They were willing and able to kill Philip for simply leaving the compound. She didn't want to find out what they would do to him if they ever found out that he was running away with her. No, she had to be careful. And that took time, preparation, and most of all: secrecy.

"But since you are here," he said, shaking his head as if to rid himself of any sentimentalities, "and because it is my last night off. Let's make the most of it. What do you say?"

He monitored the lamp on the side table, looking for a flicker. That's how he knew when she was dialled in. The light would flare from the camera's power surge when switched on and off.

"Good, you are still here," he concluded and a dangerous smile crept onto his face. "Will you also do me a favour?"

He unbuttoned his shirt, just like he did the first time she watched him. But this time it was for her, and for her alone. Her pulse quickened, watching the silken shirt fall off his muscular chest in one fluid motion.

"You know how much it turns me on... you watching me. Right?"

He spoke to her as if they had a real conversation. Sofie felt his presence right there in her little apartment, surrounding her, touching her and she whispered "yes" in reply to his question.

His triceps tightened as he unzipped his pants and let them drop to the ground.

Sofie watched his every move, mesmerized by his confidence. He was beautiful and he knew it. There was no hesitance or needless show. He was like a Greek statue, classical and understated, yet commanding in every way.

"Won't you join?"

Sofie's breath hitched. It was one thing to admire his flawless physique but quite another to admit how much he could excite her, being miles away and merely talking to her. But seeing how he lost himself in the moment was so enticing, it dragged her with him like an avalanche. In the dark of the room her hand found its way into her pants, circling through her wetness.

"Just thinking about how you were riding me... It makes me so hard."

He stroked himself slowly, savouring how the pleasure was building up. His head fell against the wall and a low rumble came from his chest.

"How you touched me..."

He let his other hand glide over his abdomen and the muscles twitch under his touch. Sofie drank in the memory of how his skin felt under her palm, its texture, how it moved over his powerful core below. She wanted to touch him again. Feel his heat. His contagious lust for pleasure.

"It felt different than with other clients. With you it was... truer. I enjoyed being with you."

Hearing him say that he loved being with her made her heart race. Her body was yearning for him. Needing his arms around her. Inhaling his scent. Sofie bit back a moan as she let a finger slide inside her.

His breathing had quickened and he picked up speed.

"I want your body to move against mine... Your breasts bounce... Your hips thrust..."

Sofie let the rhythm of his words guide her hands until she couldn't hold back any longer. With a couple of harder strikes she tumbled over the edge and waves of satisfaction made her legs tremble.

She only vaguely heard him say, "Sofie, I want you so badly," before he too found his release.

Sofie's wild heart slowly returned to normal when Philip approached the camera.

"Please, come tomorrow. Lunchtime. It's the last chance to see you before I'm... before things change."

He pressed his lips together as if there was more to say and he had to stop himself. With a frustrated groan he got up to leave. Sofie breathed a sigh of relief. He wasn't going to destroy the camera, after all. Everything was back on schedule. Just one more day. He was already halfway out the frame when he paused.

"Sofie," he whispered as if her name was torturing him.

He ran both hands through his brown hair, then turned. He was debating something and the options he considered caused a range of emotions to wash over his face. Sofie could watch the exact moment he finally made up his mind, creating a hopeful and determined expression.

"I cannot wait. I need to speak to you right now."

He grabbed the camera and the connection cut out.

Damit!

He was taking the camera apart, trying to get to the SIM. He was planning to call her on the only number he knew. 'This service is not available.' That's what he'd be hearing. She could only imagine the dismay he must be feeling right now. The helplessness of not being able to reach her. It took everything she had not to call the SIM herself.

Was it cruel? Yes. Cruel to both. But sometimes you have to be cruel to be kind. She simply could not risk Elandra discovering her plan. After what happened in the meadow, Elandra probably had his room under tight surveillance, listening to every word he spoke. If they heard them talk, even briefly, they'd never allow him to leave the compound.

Sofie rubbed the tension from her forehead. They were so close. What difference would one day make? This time tomorrow he'd be with her. Free. Starting a new life. And him being desperate might even work in her favor. He wouldn't need much persuading to leave Elandra. With that comfort she closed her laptop and went to bed.

The next day, she waited outside the restaurant. A light rain had set in but it could not dampen her spirit. This was the right place, the only unknown was the time, and Sofie was patient.

But when there was no sign of Philip, even two hours into the assumed time, Sofie felt an unnamed panic rise. What if the date Jennifer spoke about wasn't actually with Philip? Ms Hunt might be seeing her finance guy tonight? 'Our regular time in two weeks' could mean anything. This might very well be the wrong day. And if this was the wrong day, then Bamborino was the wrong place just as her research indicated.

Had she been jumping to conclusions? Getting confused by Jennifer? And foolishly put all her eggs in one basket? She should have talked to Philip yesterday. Maybe she still could. Maybe he left the SIM running. Waiting for her call. Sofie pulled out her phone. With clam fingers she dialed the number of the SIM card.

'This service is not available.'

Black dismay flooded her. This cannot be the end! She could find another client to blackmail, scheming her way back into Elandra. Just like she did with Ms. Gartner. It would take time but it could be done. She was running a mental checklist of how to get in touch with him all over again when an elegant limousine came to a halt in front of Bamborino. Like all the other times before, the paparazzi jumped to attention. Their flashlights rattled as a man in an elegant blaser stepped out of the car.

Philip!

Sofie's body relaxed. Thank god. She didn't realize how desperately she needed to see him. Needed to explain why she couldn't come. Needed him to know how much it took to stay away. But most of all she needed to hear him say 'I want you', just like he did to the camera. Only this time, she finally could say 'I want you, too'.

Philip walked around and opened the door for Ms Hunt. She smiled at the paparazzi, wearing tight leggings and a crop top that revealed her toned midriff. Her body was wrapped in a richly decorated silken sari, making her stand out as the exotic beauty she was. Her black hair was pulled back in a stylish ponytail and her skin reflected the flashlights like velvet topaz. She looked younger; the same age as Philip.

"Ms. Hunt, over here," one of the paparazzi shouted, "Who are you with, Ms. Hunt?"

"A big player in high-finance and...," she paused for dramatic effect, "my future husband."

She laughed and placed a hand on Philip's chest to show off her oversized engagement ring. Philip wrapped his arms around her and gave the camera his most radiant smile.

What? How? When? Sofie's relief evaporated into seething rage. That was Hunt's big announcement? 'I want to be seen with you', she heard Ms. Hunt's voice croon and Jennifer snicker 'It was pretty serious between them after all'. Sofie could picture the headline in tomorrow's papers: "UK's most eligible Bachelorette off the market" or "Shock-engagement: who's Ms Hunt's mystery finance god". These titles would conveniently replace the ones about the Royal Commission and how the stock value of her company may plummet.

'It's just for show,' a pathetic little voice tried to reassure her as she watched them disappear into the restaurant. Sofie could still see them through the glass tiles when Philip pulled Ms. Hunt into a more private embrace, stealing a kiss from his bride-to-be. There was no doubt. They looked like a freshly engaged couple in love.

Sofie gripped the cold wall of the house entrance to steady herself. Was this the reason Philip wanted to talk to her last night? Tell her he was getting engaged. Maybe wanting her to stop him? Claiming him for herself? She would have done it. But now it was too late. He made his decision about the future and decided that she wouldn't have any part in it.

It doesn't change anything for you!

It was hard to see the sense of that through the red rage engulfing her. But she was still a journalist. Still in pursuit of the biggest story of her career. And still in control of her future. That was her identity. No man could ever change that. Not even Philip. So, he might not need saving from Elandra anymore, but she still needed his information.

It is simpler that way.

Yes. It would be less confusing. Because now it was only work. She certainly knew how to handle work.

With a renewed determination she crossed the street, heading straight for the newly-engaged.

This feels like a date

With her heart pumping, Sofie went straight for the table where Philip and Ms. Hunt were seated. Ms. Hunt whispered something in Philip's ear and he laughed at her joke, stroking gently the back of her hand. It looked so easy and natural, like they've been lovers for years. Keeping her eyes fixed on the twosome, Sofie almost ran into a life-size chocolate statue of Annapoorna, the Hindu goddess of food. The statue's delicate bowl dislodged from one of its four hands and almost tumbled to the floor. Thousands of little chocolate grains rained over Sofie. In a tizzy, she tried to brush them off before they could leave little brown stains all over her corporate blouse. Being flustered like this was part of her original plan, impersonating one of Ms. Hunt's employees who was sent to fetch the big boss for a company emergency. What wasn't part of it, was how little she had to pretend. Seeing Philip's hand intertwined with hers was pumping red hot rage through her body.

Philip looked over to the commotion the tumbling statue had caused. He spotted Sofie and his smile dried up. His jaw clenched while he searched the room for a waiter to alert. He did not want her to interrupt his perfect little world. Well, too bad!

"Ms. Hunt," Sofie shouted in her most panicked voice, ignoring Philip's furious expression. "I need to speak to you."

Ms Hunt turned in her chair to look at Sofie, like an irritating bug about to be swatted.

"Who are you?"

Sofie hurried closer to deliver her well-rehearsed monologue, just as Philip successfully alerted the waiter. Before she could reach the table the waiter grabbed her arm, profusely mouthing apologies to Ms. Hunt while trying to drag Sofie away. His fingers dug into her flesh as she struggled against him and Philip's fist clenched at the sight. Was he distressed by how Sofie was handled or about her breaking free and spoiling his evening with Ms. Hunt?

"I work for your mother," Sofie shrieked, shaking off the waiter and sprinting to Ms. Hunt's chair. In high alert, Philip jumped off his own chair to dart around the table, trying to protect Ms. Hunt. Ignoring the pain of Philip's overnight shift in allegiance, Sofie continued with her plan.

"I work in finance, ma'am... But it was Mr. Ibuvio who sent me here tonight... to fetch you."

"You don't make any sense, girl," Ms. Hunt snapped but waved the waiter away and gestured for Philip to sit down. "Why would they send you? And why are both finance and public relations in?"

"Everyone's in, ma'am. They urgently need to fix... ahm..." Sofie glanced at Philip, pretending to search for the right word to use in front of an outsider, "...a matter. They sent me so they could get started on putting a plan together before you arrived."

"You can speak freely in front of him. He's my fiancé, now." Despite her mood Ms. Hunt could not hold back a smile. She liked having claimed him and wanted to let the world know.

"Congratulations," she said dutifully and giving Ms. Hunt the satisfaction of gawking at her enormous engagement ring. "But Mrs. Khan said not to go into specifics. In front of no one. Instead, I'm supposed to give you this."

Sofie handed over a folded paper. It was ripped out of the company's note block and had a hand scribbled message on it.

"I see," Ms Hunt huffed after reading the message while fishing for her phone.

"No," Sofie gasped, " Mr. Ibuvio said you cannot call. Not with your phone."

Ms. Hunt paused and fixed her calculating eyes on Sofie. "Ok. If it's that serious, then what's their plan?"

"Oh! I don't know, Ms Hunt," Sofie spluttered, "I wouldn't know where to begin... It's so complicated... The books are all off and the informant..."

"Are you stupid, girl?" Ms. Hunt lunged at Sofie to stop her from spilling company secrets right here. "I wouldn't ask you how to fix the issue."

Philip placed a calming hand on her arm and Ms. Hunt took a deep breath. "I'm simply asking how to get to the company. I can't just call my driver out of the parking lot without the paparazzi getting wind of it, can I?"

"Oh! Yes, of course, sorry, ma'am." Sofie scurried backwards out of reach in case Philip's influence wouldn't stop her from lashing out after all. "There's a car waiting for you out the back. If you'd follow me."

"Jasmit, don't go," Philip interjected, looking at her intently. Was he trying to warn her?

"Phil, darling," Ms. Hunt chirred. "You know my company comes first. We'll celebrate properly tomorrow. I promise."

Sofie winced at how naturally he used her first name. She wasn't a client to be kept at arm's length. And neither was he Philip, the infamous gigolo. Instead, they were Jasmit and Phil, the newly-engaged, who already knew how to bring out the best in each other.

Philip nodded and followed them through the busy kitchen to the back door where Sofie's car was waiting.

Sofie opened the back door for Ms Hunt to climb in when Philip pulled Ms Hunt back into his arms, whispering something in her ear.

"Just making sure you are safe," he explained out loud while glaring at Sofie.

He tapped against the window of the driver, indicating for him to lower the tinted glass.

"Whose company are you working for?"

"Um... Ms Hunt, sir? Is there a problem, sir?"

"Do you know her regular driver?"

"Ah, yes, sir? It's Jerome."

"Where are you driving Ms. Hunt, tonight?"

"To the headquarters, sir. It's just around the corner from here."

Sofie threw a gloating smile at Philip. She was too prepared for Philip to foil her plan like that. But her glee was short lived as she watched Ms. Hunt gliding her hand along Philip's abdomen and around his waist.

"See, it's all good, Phil. Shame, I have to go though," she whispered against his ear. "Seeing you so protective brings out the 'Sofie' in me."

Philip's eyes darted to Sofie. Was he embarrassed? No, it looked more like triumph. How on earth could he book this as a success?

"We'll have plenty of time for that," he replied, focusing back on Ms. Hunt, "You've booked up my remaining time. I am all yours from here on in."

"That you are, Phil." Ms Hunt grinned before climbing into the luxurious SUV.

Sofie was about to close the door when Ms. Hunt barked, "aren't you coming?"

"No, ma'am. I'm to make sure the press doesn't realize you're gone," she glanced at Philip as if to say 'the company isn't trusting him'.

"Fine. But don't try anything, girl. He is mine."

Sofie slammed the door shut, a little harder than needed, after hearing the exact words she had wanted to say to Ms Hunt.

"That was quite the performance, Miss Carter," Philip said evenly as the car rolled off, not giving away how he felt about his ruined engagement celebration.

"I'm not quite finished. But first..." Sofie pulled out a metal security detector. "...I need to search you for wires. For your and my sake."

He sighed but held up his arms and spread his legs.

"What was written on the paper?" he asked while Sofie swiped the detector along his body.

"They found the skeletons." Sofie paused to look up at him through her lashes. "It's what she said when you..."

"...when you spied on us. I remember. And the company paper? Where'd you get that from?"

"The receptionist gave it to me yesterday. Their coffee orders were on the other half... I suppose I never fetched them."

Philip's lip twitched. Even he had to admit how well-orchestrated and cunning her plan was.

"And you obviously prepped the driver. But she'll know it's fake as soon as she arrives at the office."

Sofie stowed the detector back in her bag. There weren't any wires. Not surprising. This was meant to be a private celebration. And Philip was never the suspect. It was Elandra.

"They're not going to the office."

Philip turned in alarm.

"Where is he taking her?"

"Relax, she's perfectly safe."

"I need a little more than that. This is my future wife, we're talking about!"

Sofie struggled to keep a calm exterior. She reeled from this final sucker punch. My future wife. He truly loved her. He wanted her to be his wife.

"The driver will instruct her to call the meeting room from the car's phone. But all she'll get on there are actors who'll keep her distracted. She won't realize that they'll be driving in the wrong direction. And when she does, it'll take time to turn the car around, especially in London traffic."

Sofie instructed the driver to head to a part of London where Ms. Hunt wouldn't dare to leave the car. And with her mobile signal blocked inside the cabin, she wouldn't have anyone to ask for help. But Philip didn't need to know that.

"So we have enough time."

"Time? For what?"

"Talking, Philip. I'm going to tell you exactly why I need the YubiKey. So you can make up your own mind. Decide for yourself what's important."

"Why now? You could have come to Elandra to tell me this earlier?" There was suddenly an edge in his voice. "Why didn't you talk to me yesterday?"

Yes, why? There was no answer to that. At least none that kept her dignity intact. After seeing them together today, she wouldn't dream of confessing that she too wanted to take him away. Offer him a way out from Elandra, like Ms. Hunt had done. Perhaps offer him her heart too, just like she did. Doing that would make it into a competition. Over a gigolo. A competition Sofie would lose. Even if he weren't in love with Ms. Hunt, someone like him would always choose the woman with the deeper pockets over a penniless journalist.

"For all I know, your room is under surveillance," she replied instead. "I can't talk about MP Kerry's crimes there. I can only speak freely out here."

"Go on then. Tell me." He sounded frustrated.

"Not here." They were standing in the back alley of the restaurant, surrounded by dumpsters and empty cardboard boxes. Their conversation was echoing off the brick walls and could probably be listened to from the street. "There is a Cuban bar just around the corner. It's more private. We can talk there." She paused to add, "Besides, I hear you got engaged. We should celebrate."

"Oh, that's rich... Even for you."

He was right and Sofie wasn't sure why she said it. The bitterness in her heart somehow needed venting. And she felt guilty about it already. She was about to apologize when he sighed, "fine, let's get that drink." Did he want to make the most of the breathing space he was given between Elandra and the engagement to Ms. Hunt?

The bar was small with round candle-lit tables and a live band in the corner. The low vibration from the bass resonated in Sofie's belly and the guitar and saxophone created the latin rhythms that made it hard to stay still. The scent of spicy food and exotic cocktails swirled around them as they took a seat in the cobblestone-clad backyard.

"This feels like the date you wanted to have," Philip remarked drly.

"But it isn't!" She wasn't going to admit that that's exactly how it was meant to feel. A date, to remind him what freedom tastes like. To convince him to come with her. To leave Elandra for her. But that was before. "Why would it be a date? We only work together, that's all!"

Philip smirked silently. She'd overdone it and Philip saw right through her bluff. Sofie's skin suddenly felt hot. If there were any more chocolate grains from the statue they'd be melting into small embarrassing puddles, just like how she was feeling. As she watched him take off his blaser to hang it over the chair, she reminded herself that it doesn't matter anymore what he thought about her because he was Ms. Hunt's. But when he rolled up the sleeves of his shirt and looked at her, he instantly transformed from Ms Hunt's future trophy husband into the casual Philip, who snuck out to meet with her in the meadow. Seeing him like this made her heart reject reason and she resented the command he still had over her body.

"I'm a journalist, Philip," she said, pushing through her insecurity, "I investigate serious crimes, political corruption, and corporate wrongdoing. The fallout from my pieces are substantial. So much so, that I have to leave the country afterwards and create a whole new identity for myself somewhere else."

"So your name isn't Sofie."

She looked at him puzzled. That's what he took from this revelation?

"No. It's not my birth name. Nor the name I write under. But it is my legal name for now."

"Until you leave and become someone else again."

"Yes..."

She didn't like where this was going. He, of all people, should know what it's like to live a pretend life, for a purpose. Besides, this wasn't the point. Getting the conversation back on track, she added, "And I'm currently investigating MP Kerry. I have evidence... that she murdered the opposition leader."

Sofie paused to search for any emotion in Philip's face. Surprise, shock, outrage, denial, remorse.

But there was nothing.

Perhaps he was a monster after all. She had been convinced he was before they've met. Before he dazzled her. Confused her. Made her fall in love with him.

If that's what he was, what would he do to her, now that she showed all her cards?

You are with me

The little Cuban bar suddenly closed in on Sofie. The music and laughter around her felt distant and out of place. Coming here was a mistake, especially with the only exit being located behind Philip. He, on the other hand, looked calm, his face, a mask that could not be interpreted. This complete lack of emotion could only mean one thing: he not only knew MP Kerry had the opposition leader murdered, he probably even helped. He was a monster like her. That's why he did not go to the police. He probably benefitted from the murder himself.

"Ok..." Sofie's voice faltered.

She could not believe how callus Philip was. She thought she knew him, at least his basic character. But she was obviously wrong. Pressing him further was her only option. Reminding him that every action had consequences.

"So you knew of the murder. But didn't tell anyone? That is... criminal, Philip. Concealing a murder is illegal."

"Hold on," he said, lifting his hands in defence, "I know he was murdered, because everybody does. It was all over the news. And it doesn't take much to assume it was for political reasons. I don't know who murdered him but you having evidence that it was MP Kerry does not surprise me. Especially knowing her. But," he shifted forward to emphasize his point, "that doesn't mean I know anything more. If I did, I would have gone to the Police."

He was lying!

"So Carl Durbing means nothing to you?"

There was a slight twitch in his jaw, when she mentioned the name he wrote in the newspaper ad. Was he nervous that she thought him an accomplice to something as heinous as this? Or was he lying because she was about to uncover how deep he was involved? Sofie reminded herself that it didn't really matter whether he was innocent or not. Not anymore. He was just an informant. And her informants were usually guilty of one crime or another. It never stopped her from collaborating with them. Neither will it this time.

He wanted to share the YubiKey, whether it was to bring Kerry to justice or serve his own dubious ploy. Finding out his motivations was something she would worry about after she secured access to MP Kerry's emails.

"You obviously know more, Phillip. Enough to know what it would mean to have one of the world's largest economies led by a person who sees herself above the law."

"Yes." His answer was swift and the twitch in his jaw had become a gnaw. His hands moved forward as if to reach out for her, but he thought better of it. "I am glad that someone stands up to her. That takes courage."

It was the most honest thing he said to her all evening, perhaps ever. He wasn't a monster. He simply wasn't prepared to risk everything for an abstract ideal. An ideal Sofie had devoted her life to. There were no companions, no relationships, no friends. Her life was duty and sacrifice. Dedicated to stamping out evil. And his acknowledgment of it meant a lot.

A sudden locomotion erupted in the bar. Engrossed in their conversation, they did not notice that the band had taken a break and guests walked to the bar for drinks. Sofie gestured to pause their conversation, while people passed their table. Without the music or conversations a tense silence sat between them. To distract herself, Sofie watched the people at the bar, though she was acutely aware how Philip's eyes wandered her face and lingered on her lips. Was he trying to make her nervous? It wasn't working. Or at least she hoped it wasn't.

"There's something missing." He took up the conversation seamlessly once the traffic had settled, as if he had just mentally reviewed the transcripts of all their past conversations. He had not been looking at her, he had been looking through her!

"You have the evidence. But you can't link it to Kerry, not in a way that would stand up in court. That's why you can't write your story... that's why you have to sit here with me." There was no trace of humor in his face. "But... you're hoping to find it in her emails. Am I right?"

His reasoning was on point. Sofie found the hitman who murdered the opposition leader. He was a small-ticket low life and would have been eliminated to tie up the loose ends, had Sofie not gotten to him first. He was willing to talk, if he got a reduced jail sentence. 30 years in prison was preferable over certain death by the hand of a fellow assassin. So, he was the evidence but the link to MP Kerry was still missing. He only interacted with one of her staff members and Sofie needed to find proof that MP Kerry ordered the hit herself or at the very least knew about it. Her emails were the most likely source for that. People are careless in casual conversations, especially the ones who fancy themselves too powerful to be touched.

"But, Miss Carter." Philip leaned forward. "I can still call you Miss Carter, right?"

Sofie nodded, swallowing down a 'or Sofie' as his arm brushed against hers on the small cast iron table.

"So, here is my problem, Miss Carter. If you find the proof in her emails. I'll be in the firing line. Everybody will know that I gave you the YubiKey." He pressed his lips together. "And we both know how that's going to end for me."

Philip might like playing with fire, but he knew very precisely where to draw the line. He was not willing to risk his life, bringing MP Kerry to justice. This was a transaction for him, not a matter of moral principle.

"That's why the key must not leave Elandra. Whatever you have to do to get access to her emails, needs to be done there. If you take the key she will know instantly and neither of us will have time to prepare for the fallout. That's why I keep inviting you back. But there is another reason," he paused to drive the next message home. "You see, Miss Carter, I need to capture the thief on video. I need to prove that it wasn't me."

Sofie was taken aback by his directness.

"And I'm supposed to be that thief?" Of course she was, but being thrown under the bus like that was a new experience for her. "How do you picture that to end for me?"

He leaned back. Calmly studying her. He heard the accusation but it did not phase him the slightest.

"That's what you are preparing for, Miss Carter, isn't it? You will uproot your life and disappear before the article is published. You'll take the consequences. Why should anyone else be impacted, if it's not necessary?"

A million thoughts raced through Sofie's mind. But his unashamed self-preservation angered her the most. She knew that her ideals were more extreme than most people's but his heartless self-interest was blatant. Sofie took a deep breath. Why was she getting upset about the moral compass of a gigolo? He was about to marry one of the richest women in the world. He reached the pinnacle of success. Why would he give that up? And as long as Sofie got access to the YubiKey, it didn't really matter what he did or didn't do.

"I suppose there isn't a need to involve you further," she concluded, looking away. "Though those other secrets in your head will impact you. There will be consequences, one day or another."

"Let that be my concern," he replied in a tone that indicated he took her jab more seriously than she'd expected. "Shall we do the exchange tomorrow?"

"Yes. Fine."

She felt frustrated.

It would be the end of their interaction and she somehow felt like a failure. She had invested too much in this man, mentally and physically to walk away unscaled. With a sigh she added, "You could have been this open when I asked you for the key the first time. It would have saved us months of dancing around."

"And miss out on your company?"

Sofie did not respond. It didn't feel like a joking matter to her.

"Look, I am in a different situation now..." he revised his answer.

"Yes. You are engaged now. To be protected by Ms. Hunt. You couldn't care less about Elandra. As far as you're concerned, that place can burn with MP Kerry once I publish my article, is that it?"

"Something like that."

There was clearly more to it. The pain in his eyes screamed for a release from an unnamed burden. But his distant stare made it clear that this conversation had ended.

He watched the band take their seats and strike the first chords of 'Save the Last Dance for Me'. With a deep breath, Philip stood and held out his hand to Sofie.

"Business's over," he said with a smile that didn't quite reach his eyes. "Let's pretend this is a date. Will you dance with me?"

She wanted to say 'no'. With business over their interactions should be over, too. After all, he was just her informant. And on top of that, a morally dubious and engaged informant. But against her better judgement, she stood up and took his hand. One dance doesn't hurt.

With a quick tuck he had her in his arms and led the cha-cha, like the highly-trained escort he was.

Feeling the music, Sofie let herself be swept up by the moment. The risky rhythm and Philip's smooth movements against her body made her feel a carefree excitement she hadn't felt in so long. She swayed her hips and savoured the glances from the other patrons in the bar. She knew they made a beautiful pair, confidently commanding the small dancing space amidst the vines and lanterns of the open air backyard.

"You can dance," Philip laughed.

He also noticed the stares around them and instinctively pulled her closer. Sofie could not help but reciprocate this strange possessiveness. It was like trying to cram all the potential future they might have had into this very moment. No one was allowed to get between them, at least for tonight.

When he sent her into an outward swing she let her free hand glide along Philip's abdomen. But unlike Ms. Hunt's touch earlier, Sofie drew a response from him. He inhaled sharply and his lips twitched.

"You're such a tease, you know that?"

He gently pulled her closer, his lips brushing over the shell of her ear. "And you are the most courageous person I know, Sofie."

She could feel his heartbeat. It was faster than their gentle rhythm would have brought on. It was matching hers.

He nudged her away from him into a turn and when their bodies met again he wrapped both arms around her waist, this time not letting go.

"I'm glad you took me away tonight," he said, touching his forehead against hers and closing his eyes for a second. "This is how I want to remember you... Remember us."

His simple statement sliced right into her heart, leaving it bleeding from a thousand cuts.

Who was she fooling? Pretending to not care that Ms. Hunt took him from her? Why was she giving him up without a fight? There was something between them. The sparks were undeniable. They had been right there from the first moment she met him. This doesn't happen very often. If she missed this chance, would there ever be another? All she wanted to do was fan this spark and see it ignite into a roaring fire. Stop being so damn controlled. Leave this moral high ground of yours and fight dirty.

"You are with me now," Sofie breathed against his skin as she tilted her head up to find his lips.

One kiss, that's all it would take to ignite the embers between them. Maybe it wasn't too late. Maybe there was a chance. Maybe this gigolo would choose the penniless journalist if given a chance.

But before she could enact her ruthless plan he abruptly let go of her.

"I'm sorry. I can't," he muttered as if he only just remembered that he was freshly engaged. "Not here."

He grabbed his jacket to leave but hesitated and looked at her.

"I'll see you tomorrow."

His face reflected his turmoil.

Confusion.

Conflict.

Temptation.

This is it

Sofie stepped into the magical world of club Elandra one more time. By now she was familiar with the proceedings. The discreet phone call. The footsteps. The reveal of the immaculately dressed companion walking down the staircase. But she wasn't prepared for her heart to still be skipping a beat when Philip touched her hand. Seeing him would never get old.

But there was something different this time. Philip's performance wasn't as smooth as usual. There was an urgency in his greeting and he turned to guide Sofie upstairs without the silent communication with the receptionist.

"Philip," the new lady at the desk called after him, slowly shaking her head when he looked.

"That's ok. Thanks, Rosie," he replied, not breaking his stride.

"What was that?" Sofie asked as they were out of earshot.

"Your medical test is missing. But we don't need it for today, do we?"

He looked at her as if to say 'there's a different risk in what we're attempting, today'.

They reached his suite and Philip swiped his card. He moved the card too quickly and the door remained locked. Why was he so anxious? He wasn't the one stealing the YubiKey on camera. Throwing her a quick glance, he tried again and this time the door opened.

As soon as she walked through the threshold he grabbed her arm and crowded her into a corner of the room.

"There are no cameras here, we can speak in private," he explained.

Feeling the warmth of his body made Sofie almost forget the reason she came here in the first place. The same intense attraction she felt the night before had taken hold of her again. Was he feeling the same?

"You don't have to do this," he whispered, as if to answer her question.

His eyes lingered on her lips, waiting for her response. When none came, he closed in, his heavy body pressing her against the wall. She could feel the vibrations in his chest as he whispered against her cheek.

"I missed you."

His hands were soft and warm and Sofie could not help but respond to them. She parted her lips and closed her eyes. His lips found hers in the kiss he denied her the day before. As she had predicted, that's all it took for the underwood of their desire to ignite into a wild uncontrollable blaze.

As their kiss deepened, he seized her thighs and lifted her up, angling her between him and the wall.

The familiarity conjured up the intense pleasure he had given her before. And her body demanded to feel it again.

A moan tumbled from her lips as his hand brushed along the outside of her legs. Reaching underneath her dress, he caressed her buttocks and she instinctively rocked her hips against him; his hardness against her softness.

Bolds of pleasure shot through her body as he gently cupped her breast and squeezed her nipples through the light fabric of her bra.

But amidst all this bliss, a small cog somewhere in Sofie's brain kept turning. Kept processing. Kept analyzing. Why was he kissing her today? After he rushed out the night before? What had changed?

"Stop," Sofie yelped breathlessly. "Let go of me, Philip."

Fury was in her eyes as he set her down and backed away. Why did she let herself be pulled in by his charm, yet again.

"She instructed you to do this. Didn't she?"

"Who?"

He sounded breathless and confused, like someone ripped out of a blissful dream.

"Ms. Hunt," Sofie hissed. "She wants to make sure I am going through with... our deal. But that's not necessary, Philip." Moving closer she whispered, "I want the key and I'm prepared to act my part in your little play."

She crossed her hands and looked down. This was embarrassing on so many levels.

"What are you talking about?"

"Oh, don't pretend, Philip. Ms. Hunt wants Kerry gone. So she asked you to make sure that I'm taking the YubiKey this time. She wants the article published yesterday. And this is how you make people do things: you seduce them."

"The deal was between us."

"Was it? Then why the sudden change? Why pretend you want me today when you wouldn't even kiss me yesterday?" She paused, giving him time to respond but he remained silent, "I tell you why, because you've talked to your fiancé since then. Isn't that right? And she has given the green light."

He looked away. Of course she was right. In some way it was a credit to him. He did not cheat on his fiancé. He was loyal to her even when Sofie was playing unfair. But that did not change the fact that he was acting on her behalf now.

"Yes, she gave me permission," he admitted. "But not for the reason you think. Jasmit has nothing to do with Kerry."

Sofie laughed. The keen collector of secrets, the man with razor sharp observation skills, who knew both women intimately, did not know about their feud? Who was he trying to fool?

"Kerry openly announced her vendetta against Ms. Hunt today," said Sofie. "She wants to personally supervise the Royal Commission because they haven't found anything on Ms. Hunt's company yet. You are telling me that your fiancé has not mentioned this?"

"No." He suddenly looked vulnerable, like he was reflecting on whether he at all knew his future wife and her motivations. "She was using me. Telling me that I needed closure. From you. Before..."

"You know what?" Sofie interrupted his stream of conscience. "Just stop! I am tired of your lies. Let's just get on with the plan and out of each other's lives."

Philip opened his mouth to reply but thought better of it.

"If that's what you want."

He forced a smile into his face and took her hand to pull her out of the blind corner to where the cameras could see them.

"Take a seat, Miss Carter. I'll get us something to drink."

He walked over to the drinks cabinet. He leaned on it for a second to steady himself, before starting to search through the assorted drinks.

"I'm sorry, Miss Carter, it seems I'm out of Champagne. Can I offer you something else. Or do you want me to quickly run down to the storage room?"

This was the opening of his play. Sofie hated improv but went along with it.

"No. Champagne is what I want. And you know how I love you going personally to make up for your mistake, instead of sending for room service."

He gave her a look as if to say 'could this be any more wooden? Just act normally!'

"Well, then. Make yourself comfortable, I'll be back in 15 minutes."

As soon as Philip closed the door behind him, Sofie was on her feet. She walked to the glass vitrine where the YubiKey was stored. It was locked. Of course. And the glass looked sturdy. She glanced around the room for a key. She didn't really expect to find one. Philip needed it to look like a genuine theft rather than a set up.

They never discussed how to steal the YubiKey. Philip clearly did not want to know anything more about this than he had to. Yet the faith he put in her abilities to get the YubiKey out of a secure cabinet and access the emails in just 15 minutes was astounding. She had to smile. But it was not unfounded.

She took out the device she brought with her and assembled it. It was a suction cap with a metal arm on it and a little diamond cutter at the end. Tracing it around in a circle sliced through the thick glass seamlessly. She pulled the suction cap and the circular glass plane came off. The opening was just large enough for her hand to reach through and grab the YubiKey.

She hesitated. Could there be a pressure sensor that triggered an alarm? Tracing around the outline she could not feel any wires so she went on instinct and pulled the key out.

Silence.

No alarm.

At least none that could be heard.

Her heartbeat drummed in her ears when she opened the laptop and stuck the YubiKey into the USB drive. She brought up MP Kerry's email account and typed in the password, "Kerry4PM". The system prompted for the second part of the authentication process and Sofie pressed the little button on the YubiKey.

"Something you know and something you have," she muttered under her breath as the account unlogged. It revealed the treasure trove of MP Kerry's emails, with three unread emails on top.

Re: Royal Commission needs to nail the bitch - We found something that will sink them: Hunt has an offshore account for a shell company...

Fwd: New funding sources - Dear Mrs Kerry, we might have a new revenue stream for your campaign. We can make it legal if we declare it as travel...

Changes to your upcoming Elandra visit. - Dear Mrs Kerry, we regret to inform you that your regular companion is not available anymore. We would like to set up...

Oh this is good already. She logged into the terminal and typed in a command for downloading the entire email folder. As soon as the data started transferring she closed her laptop. This would finish in the background and she had to concentrate on returning the YubiKey.

She glanced at her watch. If Philip's timing was on point she had less than 2 minutes left. She scrambled to her feet and placed the YubiKey back into the display. Squirting glue on the rim of the circular pane, she carefully spread it along the sharp edges of the cut glass. The last thing she needed was for the tips of her false fingerprints to be sliced or get caught in the glue. Appearance can be changed easily; fingerprints not so much. She lifted the glass in place and removed the suction cup.

When inspected closely the cut was glaringly obvious but from a distance it could easily be mistaken for a trick of light or speck of dust. She was proud of her handiwork and slid back into the seat where Philip had left her, breathing a sigh of relief.

Mission complete!

The lock on the door clicked and Philip entered with two bottles of Champagne, as promised. A flicker of confusion crossed his face as he saw her lounging leisurely on the couch.

"I hope the wait wasn't too long," he probed, dropping the bottles at the drink cabinet.

"Not at all, Philip. But it reminded me that I have another appointment today. I'm sorry but we'll have to cut this short."

She stood to gather her bag and walked towards him and the door.

So, this is it.

For all her cold determination she could not stop a hot spark flaring inside of her as their eyes met. She stepped closer, leaning into his body. Her hand slipped into the opening of his collar, feeling his skin. She drew him closer and their lips met in a hungry kiss.

One last time

"Goodby, Philip."

She broke free and hastily turned for the door.

"Wait." He caught her arm to stop her from leaving. "I'm not ready yet, Sofie," he whispered, gently turning her around.

His hand slid up her back to pull her closer for another kiss. This one wasn't passionate. This one was desperate and resigned. The last majestic flight of a dying swan.

He shut his eyes and breathed her in.

"I'll walk you down," he sighed, avoiding her eyes.

Sofie's stomach cramped when they arrived in the lobby and he held out his hand. With a casual smile he wished her farewell. He was a damn good actor. If only she could figure out which version of him was the act. But from what she knew of him, likely all of it have been the act and she never actually met the real Philip.

Let it go and move on. You got what you wanted.

As soon as Sofie arrived home she opened her laptop to look at what this grueling ordeal and fresh heartache bought her. There were more than 500,000 emails in MP Kerrie's account.

Luckily Sofie had a hint where to find the needle in this haystack. She opened the ones from the 24th of May, the date Philip specified in his ad. But all she could find was meaningless communications between her and her staff. What else could 24 and 50 stand for? Unless it wasn't 50 but something else, like 'SO'. Dammit! It's SO24, the postal code for Winchester, where she picked up Carl Durbing.

She was back to square one. But reading the equivalent of 200 books worth of emails was simply not feasible before the election. She needed to automate this. Firing up her secure messaging app, she reached out to her network.

SofiaBlack: Need a computer program to find something in a lot of text. Who can help?

It only took seconds for the "..." to pop up. Someone was replying to her message.

SlimRat: I have a new NLP algorithm. I want to tune the hyper parameters on a real-world-dataset to see what the accuracy is.

SofiaBlack: Can you say that again? In English this time?

SlimRat: I can help you. Do you know what you're looking to find in there? I can feed my software with expected keywords.

SofiaBlack: Excellent. Need to warn you: this is dangerous.

The "..." popped up and disappeared several times. SlimRat took multiple attempts to word a reply. Was SlimRat scared? Impossible, that person was just as versed in staying underground as she was. Though she never actually met SlimRat, they had teamed up on several other projects before. No, SlimRat wasn't scared, there was something distracting.

SlimRat: Not expecting a walk in the park, Sof. Send the encrypted file the usual way. I'll have something back by tomorrow, unless the news keeps distracting me. There's something big going down in England ATM.

SofiaBlack: You are a trouper. Thanks.

Sofie switched on the news to find out what SlimRat was talking about.

"The circumstances are rather dubious," the anchor announced, "A spokesperson told NewsTonight that she suffered a fatal heart attack. But why she was at the country house or who the younger man is, she was with, remains yet unknown. We now switch live to the house..."

The picture changed to a helicopter view of Elandra and the ticker at the bottom of the screen read: 'Breaking: MP Kerry found dead.'

Thank you for trying

MP Kerry's death was on every channel. The peculiar circumstances, the unknown man she was with, the chaos of leaked information, it was the perfect fodder for a media storm. With little actual information and the mystery man on the run, speculations were boiling over.

"There are no charges raised against him," stressed the police chief on Sofie's screen, "but we urge the public to report any sightings. Do not approach the man, he is considered armed and dangerous."

Sofie switched off the news. They were talking about Philip. Who else would be with her at Elandra? Given what kind of chameleon he was, she wasn't sure what to make of the circumstances. Maybe he and Ms. Hunt decided that Sofie exposing Kerry's crimes would not go far enough or was too slow. Maybe one of Kerry's other enemies murdered her at Elandra to add insult to injury. Philip might be the perpetrator like the Police assumed or an innocent bystander caught in the crossfire.

Or it was the email breach that caused all of this. Someone was cleaning up. Starting with MP Kerry before putting Philip and herself next on the hit list.

Sofie's blood ran cold. She knew how to handle herself. All she needed to do was leave earlier than planned. But Philip might not be so lucky. His safety depended on Ms. Hunt and whether she would protect him. But both of them knew the risks of playing with fire, so getting burned shouldn't come as a surprise.

With a sigh, Sofie started packing her belongings. She was renting a furnished apartment and could be out of here in an hour. Was she being overcautious? Moving her life when she didn't even know whether the murder had anything to do with her. Perhaps. But better safe than sorry. Sofie had all she needed and could write her article from anywhere now. All this place did anyways was reminding her of Philip and how he was toying with her emotions despite the miles between them.

Her eyes fell on her mobile. But what if Ms. Hunt did not protect him? What if he was innocent? Who could he turn to? Who would he ask for help?

Forget him!

She had work to do. While Kerry's death had removed the urgency from her original story, there was something much more intriguing to write: was her death linked to the opposition leader's? Did she paint a target on her back? Was there someone even more powerful and ruthless behind all of this? Seizing power after clearing out all the established players?

Sofie put the last of her clothes into the suitcase. She folded the white sundress she wore that night in the meadow. It still smelled of grass and wildflowers and she could almost feel Philip's hands on her hips gently guiding the rhythm.

Dammit!

If he was innocent, she could not just leave him out to fend for himself.

With a frustrated growl, she called the camera's SIM card. It was a longshot, but if he was in danger and abandoned by Ms. Hunt's, he would keep this lifeline open.

It hardly rang twice before Philip's voice came on.

"Hello?"

There was heavy traffic in the background and it was hard to hear his voice over the noise.

"Where are you?"

"Sofie, thank god." His voice sounded thick, and he formed his words slower. "There isn't much battery left and I need your help."

"Why aren't you with Ms. Hunt?"

"Jasmit didn't... she called off our engagement, because I was there when Kerry died! And now..." his voice trailed off.

"She has no use for you anymore. You are no longer media-friendly, are you? If anything, you make her look like a suspect."

"Yes..." he sniffed.

Was he pretending to cry?

"Sofie, you need to help me. I have no one else."

She could hear him wiping his nose. This was such bad acting. He had been more convincing in his meaningless pranks, when the stakes had been much lower. If ever there was a time to be persuasive, it would be now. He needed her to take him in, after Ms Hunt and Elandra booted him out and with the Police being on his tail.

"Why do I care?" she countered, trying to sound convincing.

But who was she kidding? She had already silently admitted that she cared, by calling him.

"Sofie, something's... wrong," he winced, ignoring her question.

"What do you mean 'wrong'? Wrong with what? You? Trying to con me again? I agree."

"I can't..." He searched for the right word to describe the sensation, "think."

Her snide sarcasm evaporated. He was serious.

"How else do you feel?"

"My whole arm is wet and everything is so ... dark."

The sniffing wasn't from bad acting or crying. His nose was running. And together with the localized sweating, restricted pupils and lower blood flow to the brain, these were the early symptoms of nerve agent poisoning.

"How did Kerry die?" Sofie asked, emphasizing each word, to let the significance of her question sink in.

"One minute she was fine... A headache... And then she couldn't breathe... I tried to help her... but there was nothing I could do."

"Did you notice a smell? Something unusual?"

He fell silent. Sofie could hear his rugged breathing above the noise of the street.

"It wasn't her usual perfume... She smelled like ... apples... or ananas, perhaps?"

MP Kerry did not die of a heart attack! She was murdered! Poisoned with Tabun. A nerve agent with a subtle fruity smell that stopped the breathing. It was used in the Iran–Iraq War and since been banned by the Chemical Weapons Convention. But it survived as a highly prized assassination weapon; virtually untraceable and deadly in even minute quantities.

It could easily be used in social settings. Unlike other nerve agents that were highly volatile, Taubin could be handled without a mask. The assassin could just wipe a drenched cloth over the victim's skin causing death within one to four hours after exposure.

"Where are you?"

Sofie could not keep the alarm out of her voice. If she was right, Philip's life was in grave danger.

"I don't know... I was at Elandra and then... I must have walked."

Judging by the heavy traffic he was near a motorway. Sofie pulled up the satellite map of Elandra's surroundings.

"What do you see?"

"Trees."

"C'mon, Philip, something unique? Anything you walked past? Or a sound you can hear?"

"I can't remember..." his voice sounded tired, "There's shouting now... goal..."

"Goal? As in soccer? Ok, so there is a sports field nearby."

According to the map there were two sports grounds within walking distance from Elandra. One with patchy green turf the other bright green, obviously synthetic.

"Can you see the soccer field? What color is it?"

"I can't."

This was like pulling teeth. He must already be in a state of confusion to offer so little help.

"Can you walk there?"

She could hear him vomit. That was her answer. Judging by how fast he was deteriorating, he would be lucky to still be alive by the time she got to him. If she found him at all, that is.

This isn't working!

"Philip, you need to go to the hospital. You are poisoned. Like Kerry. Call the ambulance. They can triangulate your phone and find you better than I can. Hang up and..."

"No!... They'll get.. I'll be..." The fear in his voice was unmistakable, even if the rest was incoherent. "Sofie, please,... you are..."

'... my only hope', she completed his unfinished sentence in her head.

"I'll find you, Philip," she said, forcing her voice to sound calm and confident.

Once again, he put an unreasonable amount of faith in her abilities. Luckily for him it wasn't completely unfounded.

Anyone in her line of work knew how to diagnose nerve agent poisoning. Some even carried an emergency pen with the antidote. These autoinjectors were top-shelf black market commodities, directly from the army. Sofie didn't have the funds or connections to obtain them, she had to make due with the individual drugs. Memorizing their dosage and administration regime. She looked over to the medical bag that was already neatly packed with the rest of her belongings. She had restocked it just days ago.

But all of her knowledge and training did not matter, if she couldn't reach Philip in time.

She searched the sports field closer to London for anything unique that could be seen from a distance.

"Do you see some sort of broadcasting tower? With lights on top?"

"No."

Her heart sank. If he was near the other field, he would be dead by the time she arrived. There were no direct roads from London. It would take more than 2 hours to get there. Time he did not have.

"Wait... yes... red lights?"

"That's it!" At least she hoped it was. "I'll be there in an hour. Hang in there, Philip. I'll check back in when I'm on my way."

She hung up, grabbed her medical kit and rushed out the door to one of the share-cars nearby. She was on the motorway out of London when she dialed Philip's number again.

"Sofie?..." his voice was weak and the traffic around him had died down, "I called, but..."

"You cannot reach me, because my number..." she started before realizing that in his current state of mind he would not understand a word she was saying. "Only I can call you. Don't worry, I'll be there soon. Have you moved?"

"I... I can't remember."

"How are you going?"

There was silence on the line. Was he contemplating her answer or did he pass out?

"Please..." His voice sounded distant as if he was too weak to hold the phone up. "Don't hang up... I... I don't want... to be... alone."

"Philip, I have to hang up. You said your battery is already drained. We need to preserve it for when I'm actually there. Otherwise I can't find you. The sports ground is too large. You need to guide me on the phone. I'll be there in 20 minutes. I'll see you soon. OK?"

"Yes..." There was resignation in his voice. "Thank you... for trying... Sofie."

He knew he was dying and hanging up on him made Sofie's heart ache. But it was the right call. Unfeeling and objective. And she was good at making those calls. She floored the gas pedal of the little hatchback and arrived at the sports ground 15 minutes later.

Jumping out of the car she dialed his number again. There was no answer. The phone kept ringing until Sofie heard his pre-recorded voice, "Please leave a message and I'll call you back." She tried again but the phone kept ringing out. This wasn't good.

He is unconscious or, worse, he might be ...

She stopped herself from going there.

He said he could only see trees, so he must be in one of the woodlands surrounding the field. The whole area was vast and deserted. It was hard to imagine that there had been a soccer match going on when she spoke to Philip first. Unless... this was at the wrong place after all. Looking around, the broadcasting tower could clearly be seen, and it's lights were yellow, not red.

"Phillip," she shouted at the top of her lungs. But there was no answer, only the pitch black darkness of the forest.

Panic rose in her. She wasn't going to find him! There had been so little time left.

Not knowing what else to do she tried to phone again. This time, the line connected.

"Philip? Can you hear me?"

"Yes." It was a grunt, he must be in pain by now too.

"I'm here, Philip! Where are you? Can you see the headlights of my car?"

"Look... to the... trees."

There were trees everywhere and Sofie realized that in his condition he wouldn't be able to guide.

"Switch on the light of your phone and wave it."

She let her eyes glide over the dark treeline, searching for the small light-source.

There!

Like a tiny glow worm dancing above the ground. It disappeared almost as soon as she'd spotted it and the line of the phone disconnected. The battery of his phone had died. But at least she had a rough direction. She sprinted towards the treeline.

There was a dark figure propped against a tree.

She found him!

But was there enough time to give him the antidote?

Together, we'll find a way

✱ * Content note: Description of treatment is purely fictional **

Sofie sank down next to Philip's slumped over figure. He was barely conscious and his breathing was slow and laboured.

"Philip, I'm here now. Let me have a look at you."

She shone the light of her phone into his eyes. His pupils were tiny needle pins even in the pitch black of the night. This was a bad sign. The Tabun poisoning had already affected his nervous system. His lungs would be next. Filling with fluids. Until he couldn't breathe. He needed a hospital, not a graduate in combat medicine from dark web university.

"You are too far gone, Philip. Let me call an ambulance. I'll stay with you. They won't hurt you."

"No!" His words barely auditable with the little breath he had left. "Let me die."

Sofie was taken aback. He fully understood his situation yet still refused professional help. What was he afraid of?

"I won't let that happen," she decided with a confidence she didn't really have. She needed to stop this neural storm, raging inside of him. And she needed to do it fast.

With the phone between her teeth for light, she rummaged through her medical bag until she found a vial with Atropine. Poking the thin membrane of the bottle, she drew up the clear liquid into a syringe.

"This will help you breathe easier."

She didn't expect a response. He was slipping in and out of unconsciousness, by the time she pinched his arm muscle and pushed the dose.

That's the easy bit. Giving him the antidote was what she dreaded.

He stirred. The drug started to circulate in his body. When he opened his eyes, his pupils were dilated and he looked like a startled cat. He took a couple of deep breaths before clenching his fist over his chest. Sofie could see the panic in his eyes, as he looked to her for help.

"What's happening to me?"

"Your heart-rate has gone up. It's the Atropine I gave you. This is good. You are responding to the drug." Sofie went back to her preparations. He couldn't lose any more time. "Try to stay calm."

His eyes followed her hands. If the effects of the Atropine wasn't unsettling him already, the various packages with needles and bandages she was laying out surely would.

"What are you doing?"

"I need to put a line into your arm for the antidote." She tried to sound matter-of-fact but her apprehension was auditable.

"Are you trained to do that?" His voice hitched and he inched away from her.

"No."

He stared at her for a second before trying to get on his feet.

"Look, I feel fine now. Just get me to a train station. I can manage from there."

Sofie put a hand on his arm to keep him in place.

"Philip, the Atropine will wear off, but the poison won't. You will be right back to where you were in about an hour. You need the antidote. And potentially another shot of Atropine later in the night to keep you going. The poison keeps on killing you until the antidote has fully neutralized it. And that'll take a couple of hours."

He looked miserable. Anyone in his situation would. No one should have to put their life into the hands of an amateur.

"Do you trust me?" Sofie asked, knowing that the answer was rightfully 'no'.

"It's all your fault." His voice was barely above a whisper. "You do realize that!"

"How so?"

"Before I met you everything was under control. The journalists I slipped information to, knew when to stop. When the risks were too high. When the truth could become deadly. But not you. You covered yourself and hung me out to dry."

Her work was hazardous. More than once, she put other people's lives in danger for the sake of her story. For justice and the greater good. But these people were usually guilty. Caught up in the net of lies and consequences they made for themselves. These people had been doomed before she got to them. And they knew it.

But Philip didn't. He didn't see this coming. Whether that's because he was innocent or ignorant was impossible to tell.

"Everything was lined up perfectly," he continued, "I had a clean way out. And then you came along. With your morals and ideals. Making me feel things I haven't... "

He went silent and his face looked pale in the harsh light of her phone.

"What?"

"I've not felt like this... ever. And I don't like it, Sofie. My life was simple before you. And now..."

Now, everything was falling apart. In just one afternoon, he was disowned by Elanda and cast out by his fiancé. He lost his whole support network. Was left to fend for himself with a lethal dose of poison in his system.

"What did you expect? A slap on the wrist?"

"I didn't expect to die, Sofie!" His tone cut through her sarcasm. "I thought Kerry would resign and that's the end of it."

He shook his head and a hopeless smile distorted his lips.

"Well, you got me into this," he said holding out his arm, "You get me out of it."

"I'll try, Philip. I certainly will try."

That was the honest answer. She knew how to do it. She had done it before, except last time it did not end so well.

The pungent smell of the alcohol wipe filled the air, as she probed his arm with her finger. He was dehydrated and it would be difficult to find the vein even for a trained professional. Her hand trembled holding the needle against his skin. She sank it into his flesh but missed the vein and Philip winced in pain.

"Shit... Shit!" It wasn't like her to curse but this called for it. "I'm sorry. I need to try again."

He did not complain and to her relief the needle went in the second time without a hitch.

"This is Pralidoxime," she explained, "The antidote. But your system cannot tolerate high dosages all at once, so I need to give you small amounts every 5 minutes over the next 30 minutes."

Philip leaned his head against the tree trunk and stared into the distance while Sofie pushed the antidote into his body. She knew the procedure was painful. The Pralidoxime was burning his veins. It usually would be mixed into a saline drip. But this was a luxury Sofie couldn't offer. All she could do was flush his blood vessels with saline solution after each dose.

"I don't feel different," he remarked when she was finally done with all 6 doses.

"It only dislodges the Tabun from your enzymes. You still have to metabolize it." Seeing his puzzled look she clarified, "It breaks down the poison so your body can get rid of it. Beyond that, it doesn't have an effect."

"How come you know so much about this?"

His face was barely visible in the dim light of the phone, but there was admiration in his eyes. She could also hear it in his voice. Most people had a romantic fascination with someone's dangerous past, especially when that someone was reformed or apparently harmless, like Sofie.

But she could not bear him looking at her like this. There was nothing romantic or admirable about her past. And his question brought back unwelcome memories. Memories she wasn't ready to deal with right now.

"I had this happen in the past," she said, trusting he would catch her tone and drop the topic.

"To yourself?"

"No, and I don't want to talk about it, ok?"

It was harsher than she intended. Certainly harsher than he deserved. But she couldn't help it. She turned away to wipe a stray tear from her eyes, hoping he wouldn't notice. It was years ago. She should be over it by now. But she still felt the pain like an open wound.

"I'm sorry for your loss," he said, placing a hand on her back.

It felt warm and reassuring. It would have put her at ease, if it wasn't for the fact that he read her like an open book, once again.

"I got to him much later," she said, feeling the need to explain herself. "That's why he died. You'll be fine Philip."

He let out a sharp breath. He had been worried. Of course he was. Learning that someone else died under similar circumstances would have phased anyone.

He did not probe further and Sofie was glad to leave the rest of her past undisturbed. They sat in silence until Sofie's phone alarm went off to start the next round of treatments.

"So, what now?" he asked, opting for a conversation to distract himself from the pain.

"After we are done with this, you need another dose in about an hour. I'll take you home with me and we'll do it there. I have a safe-house in London. We can stay there for a couple of days while we figure out what's next."

"Why are you helping me?"

"You said it yourself: you are in this situation because of me. Would be pretty heartless not to help you get out."

"You think I can get out of this?" He sounded hopeless.

"Yes, we just need to figure out who really murdered MP Kerry."

"Sofie." He reached for her hand. "I am really grateful that you believe in me. You didn't have to do this. You could have... let me die."

"And miss out on your company?"

A weak smile came into his face. She was parroting his line from yesterday.

"It was only yesterday, wasn't it? It feels like a lifetime ago."

A sudden shiver ran through his body.

"You are freezing. It's from all the fluids I'm pumping into you. It'll be warmer in the car. Do you think you can walk?"

Philip nodded and scrambled to his feet. It took them almost the full 5 minutes between injections to walk the short stretch to her car. Climbing into the back seat, Philip collapsed, exhausted and shaking.

By the time Sofie put down the syringe of the last dose, Philip had stopped shivering inside the warm car and the windows had fogged up from the condensation. It placed them into a protective bubble. Away from the world and inside a realm of their own.

"Why didn't you want to go to the hospital?"

It puzzled her why he was prepared to die, rather than receive proper care.

"The police were there way too quickly." He recalled the events. "Someone knew Kerry was going to die and called them before she even entered my room. Someone was planning all of this and wanted to make sure I had no time to run. Someone wanted to pin this on me."

"But they poisoned you too, wouldn't that have proven your innocence?"

"I don't think they meant to poison me. Kerry and I, we never... we're not physical. I never touch her, not even a handshake. She likes me to watch. Tell her how to satisfy herself. Had she not collapsed against me, I wouldn't have been exposed."

"So? Once you realized that you were poisoned, you could have safely gone to hospital. Rather than risk your life out here."

"Once I was poisoned, they needed me to disappear. What are the odds of two people having a 'heart attack' like that? Trust me, I wouldn't have made it to the hospital. And there are worse outcomes than death."

"How did you escape, if everything was so well planned?"

"I climbed over the roof when the Police were on their way up."

He went quiet, contemplating something different while dragging his fingers through the condensation on the window and leaving sad little trails behind.

"I lost everything." He choked as if he'd just realized the magnitude of his predicament. "All the sacrifices, the planning, the risks... It was all for nothing." He let his head droop against the glass. "I can't go back to Elandra. I can't access my bank accounts. I can't go back home. I have absolutely nothing left."

Sofie took his hand, interlacing her fingers with his. Their hands fit perfectly, like they were made to be together. Just like that, writing her story had lost its appeal. She didn't care anymore who murdered whom or what the consequences would be for the world. Instead, she pictured lazy Sunday mornings with Philip, hearing the leaves rustle during long walks together in the autumn forest, or kissing him on New Year's Eve. It had taken her a long time but she was finally ready to love him. All of him. With her whole heart.

"You are with me now, Philip. And together we'll find a way."

She smiled at him, even if it was too dark for him to notice. Or for her to see his response.

He is dangerous

Dawn was breaking when Sofie pulled into the driveway of her safe-house and it felt like a new beginning. The golden rays of the rising sun danced over Philip's face. He was sound asleep on the passenger seat. The tortured expression he had for most of the drive from the blinding headlights shining into his dilated pupils was finally gone and he looked peaceful. There was a subtle smile on his face. Was he dreaming?

"You are beautiful," Sofie whispered as she leaned over to brush a stray hair out of his face.

His eyes flew open and darted around the car's interior before finally settling on hers. His jaw clenched to suppress a yawn and he drew in a sharp breath.

"I must have fallen asleep."

"Yes, you slept for most of the drive. We are at the safe-house, already."

Sofie opened her door and the pungent stink of old tires and leaked motor oil nearly strangled her lungs. The tiny bungalow was right next to a scrapyard. It wasn't prime real estate but it was deserted. Exactly what they needed right now.

"It's not what you're used to, I'm afraid," she laughed, seeing his large frame crowd the dilapidated cottage. The kitchen-diner was the largest room of the house. But even so, there was barely enough space to pull out the chair from the dining table without falling onto the smelly green-corded couch in the corner. Two other rooms led off the space, but they were in even worse condition. One was missing a door, making the corridor look like a toothless grin. Mocking them.

"No, it's not..." The disquiet in his voice disclosed how much it pained him to realize what depth he had sunken to. Being stranded in a dump, without money or a way out.

"But I'm grateful... Of course," he added, collapsing on one of the shabby kitchen chairs and holding out his arm. "Can we get started with the next injections? I want to get the needle out."

He propped his head onto his free arm, occasionally rubbing his eyes with the palm of his hand. This was how he remained for the 30 minute treatment, giving Sofie only one word answers at her attempts of small-talk.

"I'm really tired. Do I take the couch here?"

"No, there's a bedroom. It's through there", she pointed to the door-less frame. "Is it ok if I duck out? You should be out of the woods and I need to clean out my old apartment."

With a brief nod he rose and disappeared into the dark room, leaving Sofie to cover their tracks.

She first returned the hire-car into the exact same spot. An audaciously placed pylon had preserved the spot and with the help of a GPS spammer it would look to the rental system as if the car never moved. If someone wanted to find her next hiding spot by tracing back from her old apartment or Elandra they would be out of luck. She next focused on scrubbing the apartment of any traces that she'd ever been there.

It was early afternoon when Sofie arrived back at the safe-house. She found Philip sitting at the kitchen table. He was wearing only his pants, with damp hair and smelling of fresh soap. For someone at the brink of death only hours ago he looked stunning. No, he looked stunning full stop.

"The shirt needed washing," he said, shifting in his chair, "and there wasn't anything else to wear."

"You look good that way," she said, deliberately brushing against his naked skin as she walked through, "How are you feeling?"

"Much better, thanks."

"You know,' she said, moving closer and letting her palm glide over his shoulder, "I can think of things to do while we wait for the shirt to dry."

"Sofie," he breathed, getting up from the chair. "Stop playing with me. I don't deserve it, at least not anymore."

"I'm not playing," she smiled, trailing kisses along his chest and feeling his body respond. "I don't have an agenda anymore. I just want to be with you."

He gently moved her back and kept her at arm's length.

"Sofie, you saved my life and I'm in your debt. But..." His tone was sharp and he waited for her to realize the change in him. "I don't intend on repaying you with sex."

What?

How could he think she wanted payment for her help?

Oh no!

Because that's what this has always been. A job. Nothing was real. He merely played the part he was supposed to play. And he was too damn good at it.

The soft morning light flooded through the window and tinged his eyes in a honey brown. It played over his chiseled form, giving him the magnificence of a marble statue. Cold and unmoving. Yet there was a heat radiating from him that screamed to Sofie his body was ready for her. Wanting her. How could this not be real?

"I don't want this to get confusing," he continued, "I need you, and there is an agenda. You said it yourself. We need to find out who murdered MP Kerry. For your story, for the country's sake and for mine."

Sofie's fist clenched. He was so close, yet completely out of reach. She inched back, gripping the table for support.

"I understand."

It sounded as numb as she felt.

"I don't think you do. But thanks for pretending," he said, running a hand through his hair in frustration. "So? How should we start? How do we find out who did it?"

Watching him put as much distance between them as the small room allowed, felt like pouring molten lava over her bare skin. She took a deep breath to settle herself. How could she have gotten this so wrong? Misread his signals so badly? But then again, she'd never been good at relationships. They bored her too quickly. No one could keep her fascination for long. And neither would have Philip. The only thing keeping her attention was her work. She would have forgotten him over the thrill of chasing another story. So why not start with that right now?

"I asked someone to sift through Kerry's emails," she replied as if nothing was amiss. "Let's see how far they got."

She opened her laptop and typed into her secure messaging app.

SofiaBlack: How did you go @SlimRat?

"You are Sofia Black?" he gasped, taking a step back from her. "That expl ains... a lot."

"Does it?"

She was flattered that Philip knew about her work. Was he a fan? A lot of people were. They wanted to meet her. Pick her brain. Hear about her stories. At least that's what the tens of thousands of comments under her article said.

"Your stories are dangerous. Had I known who you were..."

He did not finish the sentence, instead he closed his eyes and shook his head as if to say 'It doesn't matter anymore'.

"Then what?" she pressed. "What would you have changed?"

She wanted to know what he really thought about her. It was too important. Too self-indulgent. She needed to hear it. Remind her what this was about.

He fixed her in an icy stare.

"I wouldn't have engaged with you. You don't care who gets caught in the crossfire. People die while you plow through to get to the truth. No wonder you didn't stop."

"Yes," she replied sourly, "you should have stayed away. That way you could have crawled from one golden cage right into the next. Continued to be handled like an exotic creature. I'm sorry I set you free..."

The ping from her computer interrupted Sofie before she could tell him what she really thought about him moping about what he lost instead of what she'd given him back.

SlimRat: Got your link: Kerry ordered the hit. Gloated about it in 10 emails. Too bad she's dead. Would have made a good story.

SofiaBlack: Yeah. But *who* murdered her is an even bigger story.

SlimRat: I knew you'd say that, Sof. I already found lots of emails about the mystery man from the news.

Sofie glanced at Philip. He was standing by the window looking out. No doubt still fuming about her judgement over his life choices.

"I'll be in the other room."

"Sure." He did not even bother to turn around.

SofieBlack: His name is Philip...

SlimRat: That's his "stripper" name. He works for Elandra. It's a sex-club for women, can you imagine? Anyways, his real name is Philón Chase.

SofiaBlack: He was with her when she died.

SlimRat: He wasn't only with her, Sof. I think he did it.

Sofie's eyes shot up, watching Philip's back through the open door frame. Could he be a killer? If so, did he accidentally poison himself? Or was this his insane plan to get away with murder?

SofiaBlack: Why would he kill her?

SlimRat: Philón collected a lot of stock options from some big insurance company. He was planning to marry the CEO and force her to put something in the prenup that allowed him to sell those options. Kerry got wind of it. So he killed her.

SofiaBlack: I don't get it.

SlimRat: His motive was money. Selling the stocks would have made him *very* rich.

Sofie swiped her tongue over her lower lip. Philip was used to living in luxury. Gaining financial independence to keep his lifestyle after Elandra made sense. Especially if he was planning to leave Ms Hunt. But was it enough for murder?

SofiaBlack: Ok, but that's not illegal.

SlimRat: Oh, none of it is. Philón is too clever for that.

SofiaBlack: Then why did Kerry have a problem with it?

SlimRat: Putting so many options on the market would cause the price to skyrocket.

SofiaBlack: Ok? But that's the CEO's problem, not Kerry's.

SlimRat: Well, Ms. Hunt would know ways to correct the price. For her, it'd be just a temporary volatility. She might even see it as a romantic gesture to her new husband. Women can be funny that way. But for Kerry it's a big problem. The Government Bonds have shortened the stock. Probably on Kerry's recommendation and what she knew about the outcome of the Royal Commission.

SofiaBlack: So if this goes wrong the government might lose trillions.

SlimRat: Yes and Kerry needs to stop this at all costs. But before she could tell the Royal Commission about Philón's deal, he murders her.

SofiaBlack: But if Kerry feared for her life then why go to Elandra to meet with him?

SlimRat: Who says she had a choice?

A shudder ran through Sofie's body as she looked up to find Philip staring at her. Did he know they were talking about him?

SofiaBlack: He got poisoned too.

SlimRat: How do you know?

SofiaBlack: Because he's with me now.

SlimRat: What? Are you crazy? Philón is dangerous! Don't let his pretty face fool you. You need to get away from him.

SofiaBlack: You don't know him.

Sofie chewed her lips. Did she know him? She was wrong about him so many times already. He could be a murderer and she wouldn't have a clue. She watched the "..." appear and disappear while willing Philip to stay in the other room. If only there was a door to put between them.

SlimRat: I'm coming to you. Next flight leaves in an hour. I'll be in England tonight. Tell me where you are.

SofiaBlack: I'm at my safe-house. I don't need your help!

SlimRat: What do you mean you don't need my help? You took him into your safe-house, for crying out loud! You're having your arse murdered over there, babe. The hell you don't need my help!

Sofie should be fuming right now, having her judgment questioned like that, but instead there was a warm fuzzy feeling spreading inside her. SlimRat never got protective before. It was strange to think that there was a real name behind the username, and that this person cared about her.

SlimRat had been with her through some of her toughest cases. A more sentimental person would call SlimRat her best friend.

SofiaBlack: And I should trust you? Sounds like you too want to murder my arse!

SlimRat: If I was interested in any of your body parts, I would have made a move long ago. I'll send you an address. Go there NOW. I'll see you tomorrow. IRL.

Sofie closed the laptop and her smile instantly dried up. Philip, Philón or whatever his real name was stood in the door frame, examining her.

"So? What did your informant tell you about me?"

"Who says we talked about you?" She tried to look neutral, to not give him anything. But he knew. "Do you have anything you want to tell me?"

She wanted to give him a chance to explain. To lift the secrets between them. To tell her that he wasn't a murderer. But he did not reply. He just watched her.

"If you'd excuse me, I have another errand to run." It sounded ordinary and plausible, but all she wanted to do was get out. Get away from his probing eyes. "I'll be back tomorrow. There is food in the cupboard."

A dark cloud rolled over his face.

"So that's how it is now?" he said, putting his arm against the door frame to prevent her from passing. "I refuse to have sex with you, and you punish me by not trusting me anymore?"

It was a trap. He wanted her to defend herself by saying that it was the new information not the sex that made her suspicious. But she wasn't biting.

"Yes, Philip. I take rejections very badly."

"I see."

He stepped out of the way to let her leave. He must have realized that he wouldn't get anything out of her. But there was a strange fire burning in his eyes. He had just made a new plan. One that didn't require her.

Had the tables turned?

Was Sofie the curator of secrets now?

Had she become a risk that needed to be removed?

You walked out on me

Sofie's thoughts were racing as she drove away from the safe-house. She'd peeled away so many layers from Philip already, yet there seemed to be so much more to him. Was he Phil, who so desperately needed to get away from Elandra that he accepted a marriage proposal? Or was he Philón who cunningly schemed his way towards becoming a very wealthy man, leaving dead bodies in his wake? All she knew was she needed to get away from him and his charm to figure any of this out.

The sun was setting, when she arrived at the serviced apartment SlimRat had rented. It was in a posh high-rise tower overlooking the Thames. This can't be right. Sofie parked her shabby little rental in the visitor car park between a fancy Bugatti and sleek Lotus. The place must be costing a fortune, even if it was only a dingy little studio on a lower level. How could SlimRat afford this?

"Can I help you, miss?" The porter called from behind the gold-laced desk as Sofie entered the glitzy foyer.

"Yes. A friend of mine booked an apartment here. I'm a little early. But I was wondering if you could buzz me up."

"I see," he said, casting a dubious look over her clothes, "can I have the name, please?"

"I... I don't actually have a name."

Sofie felt foolish.

"Of course, you don't." His lips curled into a lopsided patronizing smile. "These friends never give their names to people like you. I think you better leave. Come back when your friend is in or better yet take your business elsewhere."

Sofie took a deep breath. He must be thinking she was a drug dealer, trying to scheme her way into the building to sell her wares.

"I have the reservation number, if that helps?"

The porter rolled his eyes, but dutifully looked over the number on Sofie's phone. He paused to check the number again before nodding with an exacerbated expression. He disapproved of her and how she'd gotten the number, but had no grounds anymore to turn her out.

"You may go up. But let me warn you: there is no other business to be had here while you wait for your friend. You are to stay in your suite. No walking around the pool or bar area. Did I make myself clear? We are a respectable establishment!"

Sofie nodded, she did not bother to correct him. Being a drug dealer wasn't the worst thing she'd been accused of today. She couldn't quite decide what hurt her more: Phillip thinking she had no regard for other people's lives or SlimRat implying her judgement was blinded by love.

The porter punched the access code into the lift's operating system and hovered until the sliding doors closed behind her. He must have had some pretty bad experiences to be so suspicious. Too much money obviously brings out the worst in people.

'Level 34,' the lift chimed and the doors opened to a vast living room overlooking London. The kitchen and lounge area had a whole wall with floor-to-ceiling window panes and the marble flooring shimmered in the setting sun. Sofie took in the breathtaking view, before exploring the rest of the apartment. She brushed against the opulent flower bouquets, lining the hallway and inhaled the crisp fresh smell of the linen that covered the enormous beds in the three adjacent bedrooms. She felt misplaced amongst all this luxury.

But Philip would fit right in.

This was his level of luxury. The standard he was used to. She looked up the spiral staircase leading to the upstairs balcony and could not help but picture him walking down. His footsteps echoing in the immense space and his scent wrapping itself around her.

The irony.

Philip was trapped in a barely liveable barrack, while she could lounge on a sofa that probably cost more than her yearly income. They truly had reversed their roles. Philip was free, while Sofie had to be protected by a wealthy benefactor and potentially had to dance to their tune.

She shook her head. This was only temporary. Only until she had figured out who to trust. Or better yet, had to trust no one again.

The elevator let out a gentle chime, announcing that someone was entering the apartment. SlimRat was coming. Sofie tried to steady her nerves. Breathing in slow deliberate breaths. What if SlimRat wasn't a philanthropist? What if whoever stepped out of the elevator wanted something from her. Something she wasn't prepared to give?

The lift doors opened and a woman in her thirties stepped out of the elevator. Her exuberant energy filled the room like a shockwave.

"Honey, I'm home!" she beamed.

Sofie was stunned how accurate the username described the figure storming towards her. 'Slim' was an understatement. She could see every tendon in the woman's bony arms. Her pink mouth barely hid the enormous square front teeth and her sharp pointy nose stood out of her face like a curious snout.

"SlimRat," Sofie exclaimed, instantly liking the bouncy person in front of her.

"Sof, how gorgeous are you?" She placed two fingers under Sofie's chin to move her head from side to side. "Look at those cheekbones." Busting out in a hearty laugh, she added, "I pictured you very differently, babe."

"Um. Me too, SlimRat," Sofie replied even though she never actually had much of a picture in her head. She didn't even know what gender SlimRat was before now.

"Really? The girls I shag always give me some rodent pet-name. Anyways, you better call me Rachel here. Rachel Pettersen. That's what I rented the apartment under. What's your offline name?"

"Sofie... at the moment."

"Sofie?" Rachel gave a snort. "That's very close... Luckily you have nothing to hide. Oh wait, you do have that murderous boyfriend of yours sitting in your safe-house," she quipped, adding more seriously, "what if he finds out who you really are? 'Sofia Black' the award-winning journo?"

"He already knows..."

Sofie looked down. It was a beginner's mistake. She should have known better. Should have protected herself better.

"Oh girl..." Rachel winced. "Why don't I freshen up a bit and then we'll have a glass of wine. You can tell me all about this Mr. Wonderful who got your head screwed on wrong. The fridge should be fully stocked."

"Thanks, Rachel."

She meant it. She needed to talk. Needed someone to assess the damage she'd done already, being so blinded by love. Needed someone to help her find a way out of this insanity.

"I'll take the Master bedroom. Since I am paying for this dig." Rachel yelled over her shoulder while grabbing her luggage and marching towards the double-door room.

When Rachel appeared again her short black hair was wet and dishevelled, giving her the charm of a drowned sewage rat.

Sofie smiled and handed Rachel a glass of chilled white wine. She was more excited than she cared to admit. It's been years since she had a relaxed night out with someone.

Rachel crooked her head.

"Are you flirting with me?" she asked with a cocky smile. "Because if you are, I need to tell you straight up that you're not my type. Sure, if you were the last woman on earth, I'd not kick you out of my bed, but luckily for both of us there are plenty more left."

"I wasn't, Rachel," Sofie laughed. "But getting a rebuff from you too rounds up the day nicely."

"I take it you are sulking over Mr. Wonderful?"

"Philip. Yes."

"Philón!" Rachel corrected her more forcefully than needed.

"Fine. Yes. Him."

"What's so special about him?"

It was a genuine question. A simple one even. But Rachel finished half her glass, waiting for Sofie's answer.

"I don't actually know," she finally admitted. "I mean, he's incredibly handsome and sex with him is..." She stopped herself seeing Rachel roll her eyes. "But it's more than that. He is smart and perceptive. He cares about people and what happens to them. And he... understands me. He somehow knows what I think."

"Geez. Knowing what you think... I wonder how difficult that is." Rachel tapped her index finger on her mouth, pretending to think hard. "Sof, I hate to break it to you but you aren't subtle. Anyone with eyes can see how bad you have it for him. He is simply exploiting that."

Sofie flinched at Rachel's brutal honesty. Maybe she had been so starved for affection that she saw them in a gigolo doing his job?

"Maybe..."

"I think you should draw a line under this and move on."

"But he's still useful for the case. He knows the players and their secrets. And he wants to help me bring them down."

"Unless he is the case. As in, the murderer?"

"Well, yes..." Sofie huffed, rubbing the bridge of her nose. "I seem to have lost all abilities to work a suspect. I simply cannot tell with him."

"Hey, don't be so hard on yourself. You've been a total robot recently. It's ok to let loose sometimes. We can work on finding you a less homicidal match in the future."

"I don't want to 'let loose', Rach. It's not who I am. Or what I do... I want to solve this case."

"Ok." Rachel's voice was soft, like talking to a startled horse. "Why don't we fetch him and talk to him together? I'm actually quite curious to meet this kryptonite of yours."

"Yes! Let's do that. Let's go now."

"Why are you excited?" Rachel's eyes narrowed. "You're dying to see him again, aren't you?"

"No," Sofie lied. "With your help I might finally get a break in the case. That's all."

It was just after nine pm when they stepped out of the apartment's rental car. The elegant black Mercedes looked out of place in front of Sofie's run-down safe-house. Long bizarrely shaped shadows from the scrapyard's flood-lights fell over the cottage, making it look like a scene from a horror movie.

"Golly, that's how you live, Sof?" Rachel kicked an empty soda can out of the way. "You definitely needed rescuing. This place is grim."

"No lights on..."

It was more a question than a statement. What happened to Philip? Why would he sit in the dark? Did she misjudge the extent of the poisoning? Had he slipped back into a coma?

"I shouldn't have left him."

Sofie sprinted towards the door. She could taste her anxiety as she fought with the rusty lock. It finally gave and the door flew open with a loud bang. Sofie tumbled into the living room. It was empty. She could picture him collapsed on the bed. Or unconscious on the bathroom floor. But both rooms were empty.

She ran through the nettles to the back of the house, cursing as their stings scratched her skin. The backyard was a deserted wasteland. Empty except for a small shed in the back. She rattled on its wooden door and glimpsed through the blind glass. No sign of Philip there either.

When she returned to the living room she shook her head.

"He's gone."

Anger and shock made her voice shake.

"Yes," said Rachel calmly, holding up a scruffy piece of paper. "But he's left you a note."

She handed her the neatly written message.

Dear Sofie,I don't know what they told you to make you walk out on me.But know one thing: I did not kill Kerry.We could have solved this together.Phil

Sofie sank onto the chair. It creaked as it took her weight. Walk out on me. Was that how he felt? That she had abandoned him? Sofie took a deep breath. At least he was ok, that was a small solace, even if she might never see him again.

Rachel placed a hand on her shoulder.

"Do you think that's Phil for Philip... or Philón?"

"Does it matter anymore?"

"Yes, Sof. If it's Philip he was just playing with you. If it's Philón he was ready to tell you the truth..."

She needed to find him before the suspense and guilt was eating her alive.

Yet another rival

What Sofie feared the most had finally happened. Philip was gone. He vanished from the safe-house, disconnected the SIM, and cut her out of his life. We could have solved this together. The possibilities of his hypothetical punched a whole in Sofie's heart. Could have..., should have..., would have... There was a lot she'd do differently, if she got the chance. Starting with asking him whether Phil stands for Phillip of Philón.

"I don't know what to believe anymore, Rach."

Sitting at the kitchen bench in Rachel's luxurious penthouse, Sofie rubbed her throbbing temples.

"Believe?" Rachel lifted an eyebrow. She hated seeing her friend turn into a spineless lump over a man. "Why is that even an option? You are a journalist. You don't believe, you find the truth. You expose it, not get caught up in it."

This enthusiastic pep-talk would have worked once. But Sofie was too tired. Physically and emotionally. She was done trying to keep up her facade. It was easy to be strong, objective, and resourceful when it was someone else's life that was falling to pieces. But this was her future. If Philip was innocent she would have wanted him in her life. Even if they were just friends. And who knows, with his free will restored he might have picked her after all. But all this possibility was taken from her, it riddled her with self-doubt, and sapped all motivation. There was nothing she wanted to do except curl up to hold the crippling emptiness in her heart at bay.

"...unless, of course," Rachel continued, ignoring Sofie's despair, "you are too afraid of the truth. Scared that the infallible judge of character was fooled by a pretty face. Like a love-sick puppy."

Sofie glared at her friend.

"Feel free to stop helping any time, Rach."

With a disappointed sigh, Rachel gave Sofie a pad on the back and got up to leave. Tough love was her only approach and it wasn't working.

It wasn't working because Sofie wasn't actually afraid of what she'd find out about Phil. She was afraid that her past was catching up with her.

"It just feels so similar...," Sofie sobbed.

Rachel stopped and turned around.

"What do you mean 'similar'? Similar to you and... Damien?"

Sofie nodded. She could hear Rachel's respect for the man and it made her stomach cramp.

"Damien died, Sof. He did not walk out on you... he would have never done that."

"How would you know?" she snapped. "You met neither of them."

Sofie took a deep breath before looking at Rachel. "I'm sorry, I didn't mean to..."

Why was she apologizing? Damien was her partner. It was her loss. She carried the emotional baggage. Not Rachel. Rachel was just a distant witness. She didn't even know the full story.

"I never told you why Damien died."

Sofie blinked the tears out of her eyes. She'd been hiding from the truth. Avoiding thinking about it. But she'd have to face her demons someday. So it might as well be today.

"I saw the warning signs. I realized how close they've gotten to us. But the story was important enough to take a risk. At least that's what I thought at the time. Now, it all seems so meaningless." Tears streamed down Sofie's face. "I've lost the man I loved. Because I kept pushing where I should have walked away. And he paid the price. For what? A jail sentence and a couple hundred words on a page?"

Her tears were hot and shameful, carving a self-deprecating grimace on her face.

"Damien was poisoned because I couldn't let go. And I made the same exact mistake again with Phil. Before I left the safehouse he said I had this insatiable hunger for the truth and didn't care for the people around me. I think he's right."

Rachel's expression softened.

"But that's what makes you so effective. You don't let fear dictate your actions. Damien admired that. It's why he was fighting for you. Why he died for you. He wouldn't have wanted you to give up. And neither does Phil. If -- and that's a big 'if' -- he is innocent, he needs someone to keep searching for the truth. And with two high-profile murders, who else is brave enough to stand up for him, if not you?"

Sofie knew her friend was right. She needed to stay on the case. Needed to investigate. Needed to help Phil get to the truth. It was her only chance to atone to him.

"Yes. You're right." Sofie dragged herself up from the kitchen island. "I'll make us some coffee, then we can review what we know so far."

"That's the spirit!"

With two steaming pots of coffee in front of them, Sofie kicked off the summary.

"Ok, so, Phil has stock options in Ms. Hunt's insurance company. He was working on getting the permission to sell them when MP Kerry died."

"You mean: when Kerry was conveniently removed from standing between him and his insane mountain of cash."

Sofie's eyes shot up at Rachel. Wasn't she also insanely rich? Why was she so hostile towards Phil's pursuits? Having disposable funds was certainly helpful in an emergency like this.

"We also know that Ms. Hunt was in on it," Rachel continued ignoring Sofie's stare, "because she agreed to marrying him."

"Yes."

Sofie flinched. It still stung to be reminded that he proposed to her. "But Kerry wasn't ok with the deal. She saw her government funds go down the drain if the deal went through."

"...so he killed her," Rachel concluded.

"We don't know that."

"Fine. So, who else could have done it?"

"Who else had something to lose if Kerry stopped the deal?"

This was how Sofie liked to approach a topic: find the central question and work backwards from there. "Who else would have wanted the stock price to go up."

"Ms. Hunt, maybe?" Rachel offered. "After all the disaster with the Royal Commission a higher company evaluation would have secured her job."

Good start. After all, she helped come up with the first part of the plan. It made Sofie furious, just thinking about the two of them together. They would have carefully planned, negotiated, and celebrated, just like they did for their engagement. So, was Ms. Hunt capable of going one step further and planning a murder behind Phil's back? Sofie clenched her fist. As much as she wanted to pin the crime on her rival, it was an unlikely scenario.

"She needed him alive for the plan to work. The risk of accidentally poisoning him was too large. The witch is way too careful."

"You really don't like her, do you?"

"There was more between them than just business. He is probably with her right now. So, no, I don't like her one bit."

"Well, worry about her later." Rachel wasn't interested in their love triangle. "You might not want him anymore after all of this is over. So, who else could have done it?"

"Someone from the company board? They would have known about the deal too. Selling such a large volume of options would require their approval."

"And they could use this opportunity to line their pockets or get more influence on the board..."

"Except," Sofie probed her own theory, "picking Elandra as the venue is odd. Why would they want to make it so public?"

"To humiliate Kerry?" Rachel tried.

"Or blackmail Phil..." Sofie said slowly. She was thinking this through as she spoke. "Yes. Why go to the stock market when you can get the shares for free by framing Phil for murder?"

"That's quite ruthless."

"Murder typically is... They also would have to know that Phillip was Philón." Sofie's eyes fell on Rachel, "How did you find that out?"

"It was in Kerry's emails. Philip and Philón had the same semantic context."

"Semantic what?" Sofie hated when Rachel used tech jargon, "What does that even mean?"

"It means that the two words either occurred in the same sentence, like 'Philip is Philón', or used interchangeably, like 'Philip works at Elandra' and 'Philón works at Elandra'."

"That's clever," Sofie admitted. "Could we use this to find other people that are connected to Phil? Maybe that leads us to the murderer?"

"Let me check." Rachel pulled out her laptop and typed a few lines. "These are the top ten names with similar semantic context."

Philip	1.0 Philón Chase	0.9 Elandra
0.9 Ms Jasmit Hunt	0.7 Mrs Ashley Kang-Jal	0.7 Ms Aalia Khan
0.3 Mr Tequan Lee	0.2 Mr James Yates	0.05 Mr Fa Ibuvio
0.03 Ms Siri Tommer	0.001	

Sofie scanned the list. Philip, Philón, Elandra and Ms. Hunt were obvious connections. Similarly, Ms. Khan and Mr. Ibuvio, the finance and public relations officer at Ms. Hunt's insurance company. What surprised her was to see Yates on this list. Wasn't he the security guard at Elandra? But according to Security he was still in an asylum, so could be ruled out.

"Who are Mrs. Kang-Jal, Mr. Lee and Ms. Tommer?" Sofie focused on the names who were new to her.

"I don't know. Maybe there is something about them on the internet?"

Rachel typed Mrs. Kang-Jal's name into the online search engine. Her eyes widened when dozens of magazine-quality pictures filled the screen, all of an asian beauty in elaborate lingerie.

"Wow."

"Ashley Kang-Jal," Sofie read out from the profile page, "Model (retired), Husband Ti Chan (online distribution markets). Rumoured to have filed for divorce this year."

"She is beautiful."

"Yes. Thanks for pointing out the obvious, Rachel." Sofie did not like the idea of such a stunner linked to Phil. "What do the scores next to the names mean? She has the same number as Ms. Hunt."

Sofie couldn't keep the anger from her voice. Had Phil a similarly intense relationship with her? How many women ready to marry him could there be?

"It just means that in Kerry's emails her name pops up as often in connection with Phil as Ms. Hunt's." Catching Sofie's anger, she added, "It doesn't mean Phil sees it that way, though."

"Whatever the connection, we won't find out by gawking at her half naked pictures. Let's move on."

Mr. Lee was next. His internet search revealed a lawyer in his fifties with various board memberships, including at Ms Hunt's company.

"Bingo!" Sofie was pleased they finally found a viable lead. "Let's see if he is the only board member who reached out to Kerry. Maybe Ms. Tommer is also in on it."

Sofie's lips thinned as the images of a young and attractive nordic business woman came up. 'Founder and HighTech Angel Investor, Siri Tommer, relocates to the UK' one of the headlines read. Sofie swallowed. She was aware that Phil's work surrounded him with wealthy women. He called them 'interesting and accomplished'. Sofie could compete with that. But it hit her just now that some of them were also absolutely dazzling.

"The score is quite low for her. This might be just a random connection. She might not even be a client of his," Rachel tried to cheer Sofie up.

"At any rate, she is not a board member. Let's focus on Mr. Lee for now and pull out all emails from him to see what we can find."

An hour later, Sofie's eyes were tired. Most of the emails she read between Mr. Lee and MP Kerry were about fundraising, lobbying events and how he despised that the government interfered with the financial system.

"I have nothing. How are you going?" she asked Rachel, who had been typing on and off for the past 20 minutes.

"I found an odd email from Elandra to Kerry, inviting her to come in to meet her new companion."

"I saw that one when I logged in. It had just arrived," Sofie recalled.

"But the thing is, it wasn't sent from Elandra's IP address. It was sent from an address that I traced back to Mr. Lee's office. The suckers did not hide all their tracks."

"Are you saying... "

"He lured her to Elandra. Yes," Rachel smiled, more at her abilities than the actual finding.

"I need to talk to Lee!"

"What? Why? You can't just rock up and say 'Excuse me, did you poison Kerry and frame my loverboy for the murder so you can steal his stock options?"

Sofie smiled.

"So you agree that Phil is innocent?"

"I still don't like the playboy but he's no murderer," Rachel grumbled. "But how are you even planning to get near Lee?"

Sofie chuckled, her mood had lifted. She had proof that Phil was innocent and there was a way forward. She would get Phil out of this mess.

"His profile said that he's the guest of honor at this FinTech party in the Tower of London. That's the perfect place for me to feel him up. Learn what drives him. What his weaknesses are. What leverage we can get against him."

"You mean FinTower?"

"You know the event?"

"Yes," an enigmatic smile played on Rachel's face, "And it's invite only."

"Ok. But you can get me in?"

"Of course I can," Rachel laughed. "But... do you have the right thing to wear? The event is next week."

"Yes." Sofie huffed. What kind of hobo did Rachel think she was? "I own a cocktail dress."

"Oh Sof, you are adorable. FinTowner requires a bit more effort than donning a black dress and putting on some makeup. It is a venetian masquerade."

That was perfect! Hiding behind a mask, she could be whatever was necessary to get his attention.

I did not need rescuing

It was the day of the highly anticipated FinTower event, where the high-rollers of the financial scene came together in an opulent night of fancy costumes and unique opportunities. Or at least that's what Sofie's invitation letter said. But she didn't care. She wasn't going for the splendor. Her objective was to sound out Mr. Lee. Find out his motives. From his emails to MP Kerry, Sofie already knew that he despised the MP for meddling with his financial empire and that he wanted to gain more control on the board by snatching up Phil's stock options. But was this enough for him to commit murder? And if so how could she prove this in a way that got Phil off the hook? That's what she's meant to find out tonight.

"Ready to shine at the 'Oscars of the finance world', where the high-rollers of...", Rachel mocked as Sofie opened the bathroom door, but she stopped mid-way through the tagline. "WOW! You clean up nicely."

Sofie was wearing an ivory slip dress with an open back. The thin straps on her shoulders held the bodice in place, but only just. When she moved, the silk slipped precariously from side to side, revealing risky side-glimpses onto her supple breasts. Her waist was tightly hugged by a black-laced waistband that accentuated her perky buttocks in a heart shape curve, flowing down the floor-length skirt.

"Looking like that," Rachel winked, "you don't need to be the last woman on earth to get into my bed."

"Stop! That's so sexist, Rachel..." Sofie scolded, though a small part of her envied the confidence her friend had. In Rachel's mind there was no doubt that women should fall over themselves to be with her, despite her looks. Maybe that's what money does, or she truly believed that charm and confidence trumps shallow beauty.

"Yeah... Play hard to get," Rachel huffed, "But, seriously, I feel like the fairy godmother, sending Cinderella out in a stunning dress to meet..."

"Prince charming? Hardly."

Sofie's stomach clenched. She was meeting Mr. Lee, who could very well be a stone cold murderer.

"You are so single minded, Sof. After your business with Lee, you could have a little fun. Couldn't you? This dress doesn't disappear at the stroke of midnight. And neither are the willing men or women for you to shag."

What a ridiculous thought. It would be unprofessional to linger after her assignment was done.

"Here," Rachel placed a condom in Sofie's handbag, "I dare you not to bring it back."

"You gotta be kidding! I won't have sex with a random stranger at a ball."

"Stop being so up-tight and live a little. Everyone will be wearing masks. It's perfectly anonymous. This is your chance to get Philón out of your head and build up a little buffer so you don't cling to the next playboy who pretends to know what you're thinking."

Sofie ground her teeth. This was way out of line. But looking at Rachel's gleeful grin, Sofie realized she was absolutely clueless how maddening her comments were.

"You know what? I really miss when I could just close the chat on you." It was impossible to stay angry at Rachel. "Luckily, I need to leave now, which is just as good."

She fastened her black lace mask, and summoned the lift. The mask gave her eyes a rogue flair and accentuated her ruby red lipstick. The reflection of a seductive temptress looked back at her in the mirrored lift doors. This will do.

It was dark by the time her limousine finally advanced to the entrance and the porter opened her door. He gaped at her daring dress before clearing his throat and mumbling, "Welcome to FinTower, ma'am. The reception is inside."

Sofie smirked. Pulling out all the stops was necessary if she had any hope of getting the attention of one of London's richest men tonight. Even if that meant playing the oldest trick in the book.

Entering the venue, she took a champagne flute from one of the roaming hostesses and surveyed the scene. The Pavillion was separated into differently themed sections. Each with a small bar and matching seating. It felt more like an expo of exclusive holiday destinations than a ball. This wasn't how she'd pictured the event. There wasn't a large dance floor or rows of gala dinner tables. She couldn't simply stroll across the room and find the person she was looking for.

Luckily they had some insider information. Rachel's connections found out that Lee would be wearing a Poseidon-themed costume. But even so, searching for a bearded man carrying a trident would not be easy. There were too many corners, nooks and little wooden cabins to find a single person amongst the 200 other guests. And after two hours of fruitless searching, Sofie needed a break.

Frustrated and with aching feed she sank into a chair at a booth that looked like the inside of a yacht. At least there was a chance for him to come here, it was the only water-themed booth around.

"What can I bring you, miss?"

A bartender in a sailor shirt that was too tight for his muscular frame leaned lazily against the bar.

"A Sea breeze, thanks."

"Right way, luv," he grinned, reaching for the mixer and the cranberry juice. "Can I also interest you in a dirty martini? It's my speciality."

"No, I'm good for now."

He mixed the drink with all the showmanship of a screeching peacock while showing off his veiny biceps at every shake of the tumbler. He splashed the cocktail in the glass with a final acrobatic crescendo and placed it in front of Sofie. His hand lingered on the glass in an attempt to summon her attention.

"How about something else later? Something more elaborate, for the lovely lady?" He was determined to not end the conversation there. "Maybe with cream? Or something stronger? I take it you are a Vodka-girl? Am I right? Yes! I do know what you're thinking, don't I?"

"Listen..."

Sofie started her rebuff when a man summoned the attention of the bartender from several seats down the counter.

"A beer, please."

He was wearing a silver mask that covered most of his face, leaving only his full lips on display. The integrated carvings depicted a fierce fox with a long scar across his eyes.

"We don't have beer," the bartender replied, not taking his eyes off Sofie. "Try the booth next door."

"Go fetch it for me, please. I can't leave, I'm meeting someone."

"Oi, mate. I'm in the middle of something here."

"Really? You think you have a chance with her?" The stranger laughed. "I suggest you reconsider your answer. You want jobs like these in future, no?"

He spoke with a slight Eastern European accent. His 'r's rolled off his tongue, giving his voice a dangerous undertone.

Sofie watched the bartender's face fall as he glared at the man. With a single sentence, the stranger had embarrassed him and put him in his place. Begrudgingly he walked over to the fridge and pulled out a beer. He set it in front of the stranger with a little too much force. It bubbled over and left a taunting puddle around the bottle.

With a lightning fast strike the stranger grabbed the bartender's shirt, holding him in an iron grip.

"Aren't you going to clean this up?"

The bartender's jaw muscles pulsed but he dutifully pulled a dishcloth out from under the desk and wiped the spilled-over beer. When he was done he wandered off with one last hoggish look at Sofie.

"Leave her in peace," the stranger mouthed towards the bartender before getting up to leave, keeping his beer untouched. He politely nodded at Sofie, before heading for the door.

"Weren't you meeting someone?" Sofie asked over her shoulder.

"Yes, but not here." His eyes trailed over her naked back before he hefted them onto her face. "I just thought you needed rescuing. Was I wrong?"

His accent turned the 'thought' into a 'sought' and 'wrong' into 'vrong'. But there was something else about him that kept Sofie spellbound.

"Where's your accent from?"

"Hungary," he replied with the fire of a Lipizzaner stud in full gallop.

"I didn't need rescuing," she said to keep the conversation going. "I could have handled him."

"Well, in a dress like that you better can."

His eyes slipped again and wandered along her body. There was disapproval in his gaze. Was he a religious person, finding her skimpy dress unchaste? A priest maybe? Sworn to celibacy, who would have to atone for lingering a moment too long on how the fabric clung to her hour-glass figure?

"But you took it upon yourself to help anyways?"

"In my culture it is considered polite to help even if it's not... how do you say? Even if the other person is capable."

"So you helped a capable maiden in distress?"

She leaned forward and predictably his gaze followed. There was something deliciously tempting in leading him astray. Was he too polite to end an agonizing conversation or was he a willing sinner?

"If I thought you were distressed, I wouldn't leave you here alone."

"Well, are you? Leaving me here alone?"

"Yes." He almost sounded relieved. "Please excuse me, I really do need to go."

Sofie watched him hurry off. In his crisp black suit he reminded her of Phillip. Is this how it's going to be? Seeing Phil in random strangers? Was he going to haunt her like that? For how long? It had been the same with Damien after his death. A small gesture, a phrase, or simply the way someone was holding their head made her think of him.

She sighed. But this time it was worse. Glimpses of Damien reminded her of the good times they had together, but Philip's shadow seemed to doom her into finding random strangers irresistible.

Watching the Hungarian walk away reminded her that she too had a job to do. She got to her feet when she watched him shake the hand of a man a couple of booths down the hall. The other man was in an elaborate costume. Blue and green fabric hung off his arms like seaweed and he had a golden trident in his hand. He looked like... Poseidon.

That's Mr. Lee.

Hurrying towards them, Sofie got her dress in order and pinched her cheeks for extra color. This was the perfect opportunity. She could open the conversation by thanking the Hungarian for rescuing her and then asking to be introduced to Mr. Lee.

But before she could catch up, they entered another booth. It was the largest one of the pavilion and the entrance to the Tower of London. Unlike the other booths, this one had two guards positioned at the entrance. The Hungarian shortly spoke to them before gesturing for Mr. Lee to walk through.

"Sorry, ma'am. This is the VIP section." The guard held out his hand to stop her as she tried to follow the two men into the Tower.

"A colleague of mine just went in. His name is Mr. Lee. I'm supposed to meet him inside."

"Sorry, ma'am," the guard repeated without even looking at her. "I really cannot let you through."

The tone in his voice made it clear that this was not negotiable. There was a secret entrance routine and she had already failed. Feeling deflated, she stepped back.

No one else was behind her or was approaching the booth. This really must be a highly exclusive section. It puzzled her how the super-wealthy managed to create a two class society even amongst their own kind.

But with Lee inside, she had no other choice than to somehow elevate herself to this level. He wasn't likely to come back out to mingle with the regular folk. So she needed to find a way to weasel her way inside, or it was game over for her tonight. Too bad she didn't hold on to the Hungarian. He seemed to be well connected and his conflicted attraction for her could have been put to good use.

Maybe she could find another willing suitor?

I have a proposition

The guard took a step forward, imposing his large frame onto Sofie. He smelled of kebab and shoe cream. He likely had multiple jobs, all of which paid too little to deal with a pesky up-shoot wanting to enter the exclusive VIP area at FinTower.

"Ma'am, you need to clear the area. Now."

The menace in his voice made it plain that he would not yield or let himself be talked into giving her access.

Dammit! Only the financial sector would sell a 10,000 Pound ticket that did not give access to all areas. But Sofie was not done yet. She stepped to the side as told, but did not leave. She pretended to call someone. It was the best excuse she could come up with for hovering around the entrance. She needed to buy herself some time. Sooner or later another VIP guest would turn up. She could pretend to know them, flirt a little and get them to let her tag along.

She could see the guard's patience run thin when finally a man in his forties approached the entrance. He was wearing a Fat-Elvis costume but his thin physique and lack of hair made it look utterly ridiculous. He either lost a bet or had a terrible temper for his entourage to dare giving him honest advice. Either way, he was the perfect mark. Sofie waved at him as he flashed his VIP ticket. The guard lifted the red corded rope from the entrance to let him pass.

"Hello," she hurried over, "I didn't expect to see you here."

She leaned forward to embrace Elvis and plant a casual kiss on each of his cheeks. She also made sure that her dress fabric strategically slipped to the side to allow him a brief glimpse on her naked breasts. It was an unspoken promise in a language he seemed to be well versed in.

"Yes. Good seeing you,... ah... Monica, was it?"

"Oh you don't remember my name? That's hurtful."

"No, no. I do, I do. You are..."

"Vivien."

There were thousands of socialites in London. Wealthy people like him would meet new girls every night, making it impossible to remember all their names. It was a believable set up for the guards to fall for, or at least go along with.

"Yes, of course, Vivien," Elvis said while dipping his cold hand into the open flaps of her dress. He felt up her obliques and moved his thin fingers up to the prize he caught a glimpse of earlier.

"Let's go in," she gasped trying to keep her smile in place.

"Oh yes, Vivien, I'm keen too..."

"Sir, I cannot let her in." The guard interjected. "She does not have a ticket."

His little black eyes shot to the guard.

"Do you know who I am?" He puffed himself up. "She's with me. Kapish? My girls come in when I say they do."

"Sir, you'll find that there are plenty of girls inside. They are vetted and briefed. Perhaps more suitable for your situation?"

"Oh well, that does sound exciting." He reluctantly removed his hand from inside her dress and gave Sofie a small slap on the bottom. "Well Vivien. Looks like I cannot take you. How about, I come back out with one of those suitable girls. Then the three of us can go somewhere else. Wait right here. Yes? It won't be long!"

"Absolutely. Hope to see you soon," she lied, feeling her stomach role as he went inside.

He was disgustingly keen. The last thing she needed was for him to come back and pester her with a threesome. She needed time to re-group and come up with a new plan to get inside. Preferable, when he was gone.

Sofie sat down at the bar closest to the VIP section. Her frustration grew with every minute that passed and she didn't have a plan. Every minute made it more likely that Mr. Lee had already left the party and it was too big of an investment to fail. Especially since catching Mr Lee in a social setting like this again would be unlikely. It was her only chance to talk to him while his guards were down. While he would not question being approached by a stranger who asked personal questions during small-talk.

Watching the entrance, she realized that she had seen plenty of people walk in, but so far, no one had come out again. Either the VIP section was packed or there was a separate exit. Maybe out the back?

Sofie was milling over her options of getting in through the back when the door of the VIP entrance opened for the first time. Oh no, was Elvis returning already? Surely his meat inspection of the working ladies inside would have taken longer than that.

Her heart skipped a beat when the Hungarian stepped out instead. His lips were thin lines, the business with Lee seemed to not have been pleasant. His eyes roamed the room and fell onto the bar. He obviously needed a drink. Heading over, he spotted her sitting at the bar and the corner of his mouth lifted into a lopsided smile.

He's a willing sinner, for sure.

He seated himself next to her at the bar.

"And," he asked, taking another look at her dress, "how many more men did you have to fend off tonight?"

"Oh... just one or two," Sofie smiled, feeling this instant attraction again.

"Do you want me to make that three?"

His mouth curved into a smile, leaving no room for interpretation.

"Please do."

She felt her cheeks flush with excitement, making it all the harder to add, "Maybe, I can fend you off inside the Tower. It would be quite fitting, wouldn't you say. I'm also curious how the VIP area looks. Do you think you could get me in?"

"Certainly," he smiled, holding out his hand for her to climb off the bar stool.

Sofie was hoping the guards had changed shifts by now. It's been at least 45 minutes since she last approached them. But when they came closer, she realized it was still the same two men.

"I'm sorry, sir. I really cannot let her in," the guard announced angrily, before the Hungarian had even a chance to speak.

"Oh. You know her?"

"Yes, sir. She tried to get in twice already."

"I see," the Hungarian muttered, looking Sofie over, probably evaluating whether she was worth the trouble.

"Well, I've just been inside and what can I say, it's the end of the night and there aren't many left." Nodding towards Sofie he added, "None like her anyways."

"Fine," the guard grumbled and stepped out of Sofie's way.

As they walked through, the Hungarian leaned in to whisper, "Sorry, that I had to imply you were a prostitute. I hope you aren't offended."

"As long as you don't think I am, I'm good."

He did not reply, instead he opened a wooden door leading into a little side room.

"There's something I want to show you", he said, stepping inside the space.

Oh no, you don't! Sofie felt adrenaline flood her system, he did think she was a prostitute. Dammit! The Hungarian was smarter than Elvis in getting her inside, but he seemed to be just as callous in taking advantage of her.

Ignoring her hesitation he felt the air with his hand.

"In ancient times, this was the cooling room. They stored beer in here for the Beefeaters on duty during hot summer days."

"Ok... That's a bit random?"

The Hungarian laughed.

"I suppose it is. Someone told me this when we were filming here. Apparently, there's a shoot straight down to the bedrock to draw up cold air.

The circulation comes from a room on the opposite side of the corridor, which sucks in hot air from outside. It's a brilliant piece of 13th century engineering."

Filming here? So he wasn't a priest! He was an actor?

He held out his hand to her. "Don't worry, I'm not that kind of person, and now I know you aren't either."

His meaning was crystal clear and Sofie felt silly for having put him in the same category as Elvis.

She stepped inside the room and a cold draft whirled around her. Within the ancient sandstone walls of the Tower of London the temperature was markedly colder than the summer air in the pavilion outside. A slight shiver ran down Sofie's spine.

With a smirk, the Hungarian took off his jacket and placed it over her shoulders.

"There. I've wanted to do this since I first saw you."

"Is the dress that bad?"

Sofie suddenly felt self-conscious. Maybe she went overboard with it. Maybe Lee would have reacted the same way? What do they say 'there needs to be something left to the imagination'. She pulled the front of his jacket closed and a whiff of his aftershave filled her nose. Phillip. Sofie shook her head. Those really expensive aftershaves all smell the same.

The Hungarian caught her gesture, misinterpreting its meaning.

"Your dress is fine," he reassured her, "just a tad... distracting."

"Distracting for what?"

"A good conversation."

He was the perfect gentleman and Sofie felt almost guilty for remembering her mission.

"Surely there is more to the VIP area than an after-hour access to a historic castle."

"Yes, there is," the Hungarian chuckled. "There's a bar. Shall we?"

They walked past several other wooden doors and narrow corridors, leading to hidden staircases and oddly shaped rooms. This place was an enormous maze, it was almost no wonder that no one came back out again. They finally arrived in a cellar vault with small seating nooks and a large bar at the end.

"Let's sit here." He pointed to a wooden corner bench lined with crimson cushions and iron lanterns surrounding the central table. It looked cosily medieval.

Sofie handed his jacket back. It was warm enough here. She surveyed the room. There were only 10 other guests, sitting at the bar or the small side tables. None of them were Elvis and his impudent orgy. She breathed a sigh of relief. In fact, it looked like a regular tavern at 2 in the morning. Sofie had expected something more extravagant, given how strict the guards were.

"Where are all the other people?"

"Most have left. This ball is a see-and-be-seen affair," he explained. "Everybody is keen to get it over with as soon as possible so they can disappear to the private parties. That's where the real fun is."

"How come you are still here then?"

"I have all the fun I need right here," he leaned back to watch his compliment land. Sofie's cheeks flushed and she had to seriously remind herself that she wasn't here for him.

"What about the man you came in with?"

"What about him?" The Hungarian was taken aback.

"Where is he? I didn't see him leave."

"He left a while ago. Out the back."

The statement hit her like a blow. She'd miss her chance. All this effort was for nothing. She got groped, intimidated and forced to deceive a nice person and now there wasn't even a payoff. If only she had caught up with them earlier or had forced her way in. It was game over for her. She took a deep breath to steady herself.

"That's a let down." The Hungarian straightened himself. "It was him you actually wanted to see, wasn't it? You were only flirting with me to get in here."

There was disappointment in his voice, but not surprise. He seemed to have experienced this before. Of course he had. Socializing with Mr. Lee, one of the richest men in London, he was likely passed over as the smaller catch several times before. Even if he probably was fairly wealthy himself. After all, he had a ticket to the VIP section.

At least, Sofie didn't need to feel conflicted anymore.

"To be honest, yes, I need to speak with Mr. Lee."

"You should have said so before. I know him well. I would have introduced you."

"I didn't know you knew Lee when we first spoke. But now that you offered... Would you know how I could get in touch with him again? It's an urgent matter."

This might be even better. Being introduced by a friend should get her to her goal faster. Especially if she could pick the Hungarian's brain before.

"An urgent matter? About what?"

"I need to ask him a couple of questions about a mutual acquaintance of ours."

He mustered her. His dark eyes were hooded by the mask, making it impossible to tell what he was thinking. When he spoke again there was a risky edge to his voice.

"Well in that case, I have a proposition for you."

Do you want him back?

The Hungarian leaned forward. There was a dangerous smile on his lips. He liked where this was going. Within the space of two heartbeats, he managed to turn a disappointment into an opportunity. He slowly lifted his scotch to toast to this change of direction before taking a satisfied gulp. Sofie suddenly felt dread, she wasn't quite so sure his proposition was mutual.

"I'm meeting Mr. Lee tomorrow. And I need..." the Hungarian lightly tapped the table with his index finger searching for the right word, "... a witness."

"A witness? For what?"

"Signing a contract."

A strange inflection in his voice made the statement sound like a question. The meeting tomorrow wasn't a simple business transaction. There was something more to it. Something sinister. Sofie didn't particularly care about the predicament the Hungarian was in, but witnessing an unsavoury deal between him and Mr. Lee was just the kind of incriminating intel she was after. So this was a mutual opportunity after all.

"I can do that," she grinned.

"Great."

There was sarcasm in his tone. An accusation. Like she was colluding with Lee to rip him off. The deal was rotten and he felt pressured into it. That's why he looked so displeased when he left the VIP area earlier.

"Mr. Lee wants to keep this confidential," he continued, "and... unofficial. So he needs a special kind of witness. Can you be that?"

"I can be whoever you want me to be."

As soon as the words were out of her mouth she regretted them. She did not mean to sound so seductive.

"Yes... You obviously are no stranger to lying. You strike me as someone who always gets what she wants."

Sofie closed her eyes for a second to take a deep breath. Maybe she was, maybe she wasn't. And why did she even care what this stranger thought about her? At least he was honest. A character trait she actually appreciated after having spent too much time with Philip and his polite but calculated lies.

Realizing she wasn't going to correct him, he pulled his mouth in a lop-sided expression. "Lee wants me to put skin in the game. I need to bring someone... personal to me."

This deal was dangerous! And the stakes must be very high for him to even agree to this. He was forced to put a loved-one in danger. No wonder he wanted a decoy. Wanted to use a stranger to act the part.

"You aren't looking for a witness," Sofie said slowly, "Mr. Lee wants collateral if things go south."

"Yes," he admitted. Was there guilt in his voice? "But I don't intend to break the contract. You'll be safe."

"Of course, I am. Just as safe as your real loved-ones sitting at home." She did not hide the ridicule. "So? Who am I playing? Your sister? Or cousin?"

"No, Lee knows my family. You need to be my..." he looked as if he had just swallowed a fly, "...mistress."

"Oh? Mistress? So you are married, then?"

He did not reply. He did not need to. The way he chewed on his lips told Sofie that there was someone, even though he had no ring on his finger. No wonder he was beating himself up over looking at her that way earlier.

"And do you normally have mistresses?"

"No."

"Really? Someone rich and handsome, working in the film industry? You must get tempted? Is that what Mr. Lee has on you?"

"I don't have mistresses," he said with a conviction that made orthodox priests look like sinners in comparison.

Intriguing.

He was the polar opposite to Philip. Conservative and outspoken. With him, Sofie knew exactly where she was at. With him, she was the one in control. Wrapping him around her finger, thinking two steps ahead. This was what she needed to get over the spell Philip had put her under. To regain her sovereignty. To get back to normal. Rachel was right!

"Well, you'll have a mistress now."

"Oh yes? I don't think you can be that persuasive."

His accent had become thicker. There was no doubt that her wicked smile had the intended effect.

"Follow me and we'll find out." Sofie got up and held out a hand for him.

"I can't." He looked torn, but with a firm shake of his head he summoned conviction. "Look, I don't know why I said it. I'm sure you'll be very convincing tomorrow."

"Listen," she placed both hands on the table, "if this deal has such high stakes, Mr. Lee won't take any chances. He'll be looking for clues. And us behaving like perfect strangers because we've never even touched. It will betray us. He'll know you brought a decoy." She leaned forward and lowered her voice. "And then what? Do you think he'll let us simply walk away?"

"Sof... -ar, as I can tell he might," he stuttered, before regaining his resolve. "Let's not make this complicated."

"What's complicated about it? You were flirting with me before. What's changed?"

"Nothing has changed..." He paused. "You have your agenda. I have mine. Let's leave it at that."

"Your agenda was to pick up a girl to play your mistress tomorrow. Well, here I am. "

He looked down. This conversation was not going the way he had planned.

"You are making this difficult."

"Yes! Because I see the risks!"

She paused until he looked up at her.

"I want to meet Mr. Lee. And I'm willing to take the risks. I'm not judging you. I'm sure you have good reasons for setting the deal up this way. All I'm asking is to not go in unprepared." She caressed the back of his hand. It was warm and soft. "If it helps us act more believable tomorrow, get your deal done with less risk, then what's the danger?" She held out her hand again. "It'll be our secret."

His expression softened. With a sigh he took her hand and reluctantly followed her out the bar and down the hall. Sofie opened the door opposite the cool room. A warm breeze whirled around her dress, tussling her hair and stroking her skin like invisible hands. Little goosebumps formed on her arms as she turned to the Hungarian. She reached up to her mask to loosen the knot and let it fall to the cobblestone floor.

"Kiss me."

His jaw muscles pulsed. He was not pleased with her demand but he complied. Stepping forward, he cupped her cheeks and brushed his lips against hers. The silver metal of the fox mask touched Sofie's cheekbones. It felt smooth and warm from his skin below. Sofie leaned in for more but he had already dropped his hands and taken two steps back.

A frustrated snarl built in Sofie's throat

"See? That's what I mean. How is this believable?"

"We won't have to kiss in front of him."

"No. But you are avoiding my touch! That's what's not believable. You'll have to try a little harder than that." She closed the distance between them. "So drop that damn mask and kiss me properly."

She reached for his face but he caught her hands.

"No. I can't let you see my face."

His accent made his vowels stretch, giving the statement an eerie ring.

"What? Is it burned? Or scared?" She paused, how naive was this man? "Don't you think that's a dead giveaway? Me seeing your disfigured face for the first time tomorrow. Or will you be wearing a mask then too?"

"No, I won't. And it's not that."

"Oh... " Realization kicked in. "You are someone famous then! You are from the film-industry and I would recognize your face. Is that it? You're an actor!"

More determined, she reached for the mask again. But before she could unveil his identity he had her pinned against the wall, wrists captured on either side of her body by his unshakable hands. He glared at her with his heart hammering in his chest. His objections came out as an unintelligible growl and were overthrown by him kissing her, rough and desperate, like someone who had just bent to her will.

"Is that what you want?"

"Yes!" Sofie breathed, desire rushed her down a one way street.

She didn't need to know who he was anymore. In all likelihood, he was a celebrity trying to hide his shady deals with Lee. Some petty crimes, which Sofie didn't care about. What she did care about was how good his lips felt on hers.

He gently lifted her arms above her head and held them with one hand against the wall. He wasn't trusting her with the mask but he also couldn't resist roaming her body with his other hand. He let his fingers trail down her arm, across her collarbone and lightly squeeze her full breasts.

Sofie moaned as his thumb brushed against her nipple. With her hands caught she could only use her leg to pull him closer, tilting her hips up to press his hardness against her aching heat.

"We need to stop," he rasped breathlessly, "I don't have a condom."

"I have one." Sofie trailed kisses along his jawbone, "I'll fetch it, if you let me go."

He let go of her hands and stepped back. Sofie reached into her handbag to pull out the foil pack, when she noticed the look in his eyes.

"You came prepared!" He let the incriminating statement linger. "Was that for Lee?"

"No!" Sofie was offended by his implication, " Of course not! A friend of mine put it in my bag. I wasn't going to use it. But she thought..." Anger entered her voice. "That I needed to get over someone."

"And? Do you?"

"I don't know."

It sounded more melancholic than she had expected. She looked up at the Hungarian. Was there pity in his eyes? How dare he. She was prepared to counter with a flippant comment, when he reached out to brush a strain of hair out of her face.

"Do you want him back?"

What the hell? This wasn't turning into a therapy session, not on her watch.

"Just shut up and fuck me," she snapped.

With that one sentence she had bared her soul to him. She was at her wits' end. Had abandoned manners and reason. And reached the end of her patients. All she wanted was to numb the heartache by hooking up with a stranger.

When she looked at him again the pity was gone, replaced by understanding and... lust.

He kissed her. This time he didn't capture her hands and let them freely roam his body. Sofie unbuttoned his shirt to let her palms glide up his broad chest. But before she could feel his skin he stopped her. He gently turned her body around, placing her hands against the wall. He was not going to let her undress him, neither the mask nor the shirt.

Standing behind her, he kissed her shoulders and let his fingers trail down the groove of her spine. Goosebumps erupted like silent explosions across her body. His hands dipped into the loosely hanging fabric of her slip dress, gliding up her stomach and over her bare breasts. The warmth of his skin was a soothing balm that made her crave for more. She stemmed her hands on the wall and swayed back against the bulge in his pants.

He kissed her back while gathering the silken fabric in his fist to expose her buttocks. Hooking his thumbs into Sofie's drenched panties, he bent down to help her step out of them. When he moved back up he trailed a finger along the inside of her legs. The suspense was putting her senses on edge.

Sofie's pulse quickened in anticipation as he ripped open the foil package. He moved the head of his erection along her slick folds to spread the moisture before finally pushing into her. He stilled for a second, breathing against her shoulders and holding her in a gentle embrace.

But Sofie rocked against him, needing more. Sensing her impatiens, he let his hand glide to the centre of her vee and started stroking her. The rhythm matching his steady pumps. His other hand cupped her breast, sending greedy quivers to her core.

Sofie gripped the wall harder. She had expected a mindless pounding. Something that would have reminded her that she didn't need physical intimacy. But this was good. Too good. It made her realize how much she missed Philip. How much she wanted him back.

As the Hungarian picked up the pace, Sofie surrendered her body to the waves of pleasure.

"Keep going, Philip. I am so close..." she moaned.

It was barely audible but a grunt behind her disclosed that the stranger had heard it. But Sofie didn't care. She climaxed with Philip's name on her lips.

"I think your friend is wrong," the Hungarian said as their breathing had settled and Sofie was putting her dress back in order.

"About what?"

"Hooking up with someone else will not help you get over him."

She threw an acid glance his way. Even if she had come to the exact same conclusion, it was not his comment to make.

"Maybe," he continued, "it would help if we saw more of each other? Tomorrow, after the meeting?"

She highly doubted that. Yes, he was good. But he wasn't Philip. That spot in her heart was already taken. And she wasn't going to give it up until he surrendered it.

Is sex better with love? That was one of the first questions she asked Philip when they first met. And now she knew without a doubt that the answer was 'Yes'.

What did you do to her?

Sofie entered the hotel where the Hungarian had arranged for them to meet with Mr. Lee. She was curious to find out who the mysterious stranger was, even if seeing him without a mask would drive home what they've done the night before. Would amplify her guilt. She betrayed Philip. Physically and emotionally. She wanted to stamp him out from her heart, but all she managed to do was burn him in deeper. It made her realize how much she needed him. And how important today would be. If everything went well, she would walk out with the intel she needed to prove Philip's innocence and potentially get him back in her life. Then, what happened between her and the Hungarian would become nothing more than a dirty little secret, no one needed to know about.

Sofie felt a mix of anticipation and trepidation as she followed the maître d'hôtel to a private lunch room on the upper level.

"The lady has arrived, Mr. Lee," the maître announced as he opened the heavy felted door. "May we start the lunch service, sir?"

With a dismissive wave Lee gestured for the host to leave and close the door behind Sofie. He sat at the head of the table and his strangely pale eyes judged her, like an eagle would estimate the distance to his prey. His dark hair shimmered blue in the midday sun. It made him stand out like a visual anomaly in the otherwise warmly decorated room.

Despite the light and airy feel of the space, towering over the roofs of London, Sofie felt trapped. Starved of oxygen. Lee was a predator. Experienced and remorseless. He would not be fooled easily. If they set even the slighted foot wrong, Lee would know. And he would not let her walk out of here unharmed.

Her gaze escaped to the Hungarian who sat next to Mr. Lee. His back was towards her and he seemed to be staring out the window. Lost in his own world, not even noticing her. I am his mistress. I love him. Despite the guilt, she was glad that she formed some kind of bond with him last night. He had been a good lover. Gentle and skilled. At least, that was something to cling to while she was stuck in this fighting arena with the two opponents. If things went downhill he might come to her aid.

"My love," the Hungarian suddenly said, still facing the other way. His voice sounded different. Gone was his accent. It was replaced by a tone that was oh-so familiar. The man turning to welcome Sofie as his mistress was... Philip.

He was fully recovered and he looked good; someone was taking care of him. Giving him resources, sheltering him from the Police and making his life comfortable. The excitement of seeing him again all too quickly evaporated into hot anger. He was back with Ms. Hunt! Back to his old self of trickery and scheming. He seduced her to come here today, even if it wasn't necessary. All he needed to do was ask. She would have followed him. Stood right beside him, no matter the risks. What was it with this man and his games? But more importantly, what was it with her and not being able to resist him? Why was she throwing herself at him? Disguised or otherwise?

Sofie focused her mind, there was more at stake than her emotions. She fixed a smile on her face and stepped forward to greet him.

"Who are you today?" she hissed through the fake smile, "Phillip, the Hungarian, or Philón?"

"You'll see."

It was loud enough for Mr. Lee to hear, but that didn't seem to concern him. He wrapped his arms around her and silenced any further questions with a kiss. For a brief second Sofie's worries melted away. She knew this looked real, because it felt real. This inexplicable pull towards him that defied rhyme or reason consumed her once again.

Mr. Lee cleared his throat, "What did she ask?"

"Who you are," Philón replied, without taking his eyes off Sofie. "I asked her here on a lunch date, so this is a bit... unexpected. I'm sorry, darling."

"Philón, Philón, Philón," Lee scolded, "you either haven't quite grasped your situation or you think that your Mistress will love you even without your money. Which is it?"

Sofie looked at Philón. None of this made any sense. Especially the expression that crept into Philón's face. Was it doubt? Insecurity? Shame?

"Oh dear," Mr. Lee laughed. He had noticed it too. "Looks like we'll find out together. I wonder how your bird will react to your news?"

He gestured for her to sit next to him. He had already decided what the outcome would be. "What's your name, little bird?"

"It's either 'Darling' or 'The Ex', depending on what this is. Philón, what's going on here?"

"Hoho, feisty," Lee muttered, "I'll definitely take you home."

"You better sit down." He pulled out a chair next to him and away from Lee. "You remember the stocks I was marrying Ms Hunt for?"

This casually uttered sentence sucked the air from Sofie's lungs. He finally confirmed what she was so desperately hoping for. The marriage was fake! He didn't love Ms Hunt. He only did it for the money. Or... Or was that just the thing to say to a Mistress? He didn't bring Ms Hunt here today, did he? Didn't put her in harm's way. He brought Sofie. Was that because he loved Ms Hunt too much or because he trusted Sofie more? The only thing that wasn't in doubt was his faith in Sofie's ability to figure out this background herself. The credence that none of this would surprise her.

"Yes. You were going to sell them," she said, playing along. "So you can be with me."

It felt good to say this out loud, even if it was only pretend. Or was it? When she looked into his eyes, there was warmth and joy. He liked hearing it, just as much as she liked saying it. A genuine smile had snuck into his face, but it died with his reply.

"Yes, that was my plan. But now, I'll have to sign some of them over to Mr. Lee. It'll still be enough for us to live comfortably. Just not in luxury, as I had planned."

"Why?"

Sofie glanced at Lee. He leaned back to enjoy this spectacle unfold.

"He has offered to help me with my current situation."

Was there an accusation in Phil's tone? I have to do this because you abandoned me? Or was this her guilt putting words in his mouth? Ignoring her insecurities, Sofie continued acting her part.

"With the police?" She turned to Mr. Lee. "Oh, so you know who really killed MP Kerry?"

"Your Mistress is exceptionally well informed, Philón. How cute. Well, let me be equally frank with her: Yes I do, and for my help I'm taking all his stocks."

Lee's lips curled into a smirk as he scratched his wispy beard and watched the bombshell land. Philón did not see this coming and the shock was written all over his face.

"Oh... And one more thing: you need to call off your wedding. You'll keep working at Elandra... as my informant." He gave a bored wave towards Sofie. "You can keep your little floosie. Smart choice, bringing her instead of your fiancé."

Philón rubbed a thumb over his forehead, the pressure leaving angry red marks behind. Judging from his chagrin expression, he contemplated accepting even these escalated terms. He seemed convinced that there was no other way out even if he was frantically searching for one.

It was Sofie's chance to take over the conversation. Maybe she could help turn the tables and get Philón out of this one-sided deal.

"How exactly do you plan to help Philón?"

Lee looked at her amused, like she had just performed an adorable little trick.

"I have information that will put the police on a different lead. One that points away from Philón."

"And you want payment for that? For doing your civil duty? Mr. Lee, having knowledge of a crime and not reporting it is a felony."

Lee's eyes darkened. He obviously saw himself above the law, as the puppeteer, holding the strings. He did not care what Sofie considered legal or illegal.

"You can have all the stocks," Philón interrupted, "but I'm not betraying my clients to you."

"How noble. But that's not the deal I'm offering. You see, I'm not actually interested in your stocks." He sounded smug, "I'm wealthy enough. There are only so many summer houses, hotels and yachts one can buy before it gets boring. But it would be a big deal for you." He leaned forward. "I cannot allow that. I want you to keep working at Elandra. Because what I am interested in is protecting my wealth. And for that, I need insider information, which you will get me."

The hopelessness of the situation was sinking in and drained all color from Philón's face. With a satisfied smile, Lee turned back to Sofie. "And for you and your little threat: The information I have might be just a rumour, or worse a defamation. I could even get sued. And who wants to waste precious police resources, when they already have the right man?" He nodded towards Philón.

"If it's so circumstantial, why would the police drop the charges against Philón?"

"Listen," Lee banged his first on the table. It must have been a long time since anyone spoke back at him, "I want Phillip to work, ok? So I'll make sure the police stops chasing him. I have my ways."

Oh yes? Tell me more? This was exactly the information she was after. The incriminating details that would be his downfall. Sofie had licked blood. She was about to sink her teeth in, when Philón placed a hand on her arm, just like he did with Ms Hunt.

"Where are the papers to sign?"

"Excellent choice, Philón. For a second there I thought you wanted to make this... interesting." Mr. Lee pulled out a form from his briefcase. "The account details are already filled in. All I need is your signature."

As Philón scanned the document, Lee stared at Sofie. No doubt going through how he would have tortured her had Philón not yielded.

"Wait." Sofie gasped as Philón reached for the pen. "You didn't kill Kerry." She left the subtext of 'I know that now' unspoken. "The police might find this out too." Or get help finding it.

A subtle nod confirmed that he understood her meaning. That he heard her offer to help loud and clear.

"Gosh," Lee interjected, "you are so naive, 'Darling'. I take it you are still 'Darling'? The police have a suspect. They want to clear this one off the books quickly. Especially with such a prominent victim and such a suitably shady suspect. Who would take an interest in clearing his name? The Ms. Hunts of the world? Certainly not. And I hear Elandra already has a new Primo. So get that into your pretty little head: No one. Cares. About. Him. At least no one important who could actually help."

Turning to Philón he added, "And you my friend have work to do getting back to the top. The women who's secrets I need will not settle for second best. They want Elandra's Primo."

Philón took a deep breath before signing the papers. "It's just money"

"No. It's not. It's your body and conscience, too." Sofie brooded. He clearly had more faith in Mr Lee's ability to help than hers.

"Well, we'll see about that." Phil looked at Lee. "You might find that I don't have any relevant secrets. Most things are so circumstantial anyways and I wouldn't want you to get sued."

With a nod, Mr Lee stood from his chair.

"Philón." His tone was condescending, like talking to a naughty schoolboy, "I'm sure we'll find incentives. Something that makes you re-evaluate your threshold for what you consider circumstantial."

Before he had finished his sentence he pulled a syringe from his pocket and jabbed it into Sofie's shoulder. He pushed the plunger and the clear liquid shot into her muscles as she let out a pained cry.

In an instant, Philón pulled Lee away from Sofie and pinned him against the wall.

"She had nothing to do with this," he seethed, pressing his arm into Lee's throat "What did you do to her?"

Before Lee was forced to answer, the room crawled with security guards. Two men seized Philón and kicked in his knees to make him crouch in front of Lee.

"You do care about that one, don't you?" Lee coughed out a surprised laugh. "Well, you'll find out what I injected after you give me the first secret. I reckon she has about a week."

He looked to Sofie while straightening his blazer.

"It'll start with a light headache, darling."

You got your answer

S ofie held her throbbing arm. *You have a week.* She could feel the cold liquid Mr. Lee injected. It was spreading underneath her skin, infiltrating her body. What did he give her? A poison? A disease? A chemical? Whatever it was she needed to know. And the only way to find out was hinging on Phil to give up his secrets.

"I don't need a week." Phil struggled against the two bodyguards who had him headlocked on the ground. "You can have what you want. Right now. Just tell me how to save her."

"I'm glad to hear that, Philón."

Lee gave a casual nod to the bodyguards to release their captive. The goons stepped back but not without giving Phil one last shove. It put a spiteful grin on Lee's face. When Phil struggled to his feet, Lee walked over to Sofie. He brushed the back of his hand along her cheekbones, wanting to provoke another outburst from Phil. "It would have been a shame to let this one die."

A low growl came from Phil's throat as he positioned himself between Lee and Sofie.

"What information do you want?"

Lee squinted his eyes, thinking about all the juicy secrets that were at his fingertips.

"Tell me about... Siri Tommer."

"She founded several HighTech companies," Phil replied without missing a beat, "She took a healthy profit from them and now invests into other tech businesses."

"Don't play dumb. That's public information. I want to know what she tells you after you've banged her."

Phil rubbed his twitching fingertips. The disrespectful statement was offending him and he itched to punch Lee again. But instead he settled for, "Why would she be a client of mine?"

Lee laughed and turned for the door.

"Sure, we can play it that way, if you prefer. But remember... it's only a week before your little bird loses its chirp."

The cruelty of his casual thread eerily hung in the air, when Sofie placed a hand on Phil's arm to get his attention.

"Don't worry, I'll make this right," he reassured her before calling after Lee. "Wait! You're right. She's a client and I have more on her."

"No, Phil," Sofie whispered. "There is no need."

"What do you mean?"

Phil's eyes darted between Sofie and Lee.

"He's bluffing," she spat, looking straight at Lee, who stared back at her in disbelief.

"How can you be sure?"

"It starts in a week?" she quipped. "That's utter nonsense. Most poisons or chemicals act straight away. Sure, pathogens can take a week. But they can't be carried around like that. They need to be refrigerated or kept in an incubator. No. It's a harmless saline solution, that's all he injected." Taunting Lee directly, she added, "and it starts with a headache? C'mon. You picked the most common symptom. I probably get one during your arbitrary one week deadline from -- I don't know -- stressing over an injection. And if I do, chances are I'll put pressure on Phil to give you what you wanted. That's your master plan, isn't it?"

Lee's expression changed. It was too subtle for Sofie to read but Phil picked up on it easily.

"Yes, she's right! You were bluffing."

"Suite yourself," Lee grumbled.

"Hang on." A worried expression crept into Phil's face. "The injection might have been harmless, but there's something else... Something you're not telling us." He studied Lee a little longer before turning to Sofie, "but I don't know what it is and I don't want to gamble with your life, Sofie."

He took a deep breath, before fixing Lee in a cold stare.

"Siri is moving to the UK. She has accepted a position at the Reserve Bank. She will be the Assistant Governor for Financial Markets. Regulating the flow of money for investors."

"Kicking out old Rodney?" Lee was pleasantly surprised. "That's interesting. Very interesting, indeed." He paused to muster Phil, "And I take it she's fond of your services."

Phil looked to the ceiling and let out a resigned breath.

"Yes."

"Splendid! I see we have an understanding here. Make her a regular, will you?"

Phil swallowed hard, trying to get rid of the distaste.

"You got what you wanted. Now tell me what the injection was about."

"All in good time. I need to verify that the information you've given me is correct." Grinning at Sofie Lee added, "she has a week, just like I said."

Satisfied, he headed for the door. With his hand hovering over the handle he turned, "Oh and Philón, there is no point in being clever with me in the future. I know more than you think." He gave Sofie a sideways glance. "For example, I know about Ashley Kang-Jal and that she left her husband for our lover boy here."

Sofie pressed her lips together. So Rachel's software was right in ranking Ashely and Ms. Hunt the same. Had Ashely been his backup in case Ms. Hunt did not come through? Or was there more? Was she his real mistress?

Sofie sank to a chair, as soon as the last of Lee's bodyguards left the room. The problems and implications were getting to her, were draining all her energy.

"How are you feeling?"

Phil placed a hesitant hand on her shoulder.

"I'm fine," she lied.

Physically she was, but the secrets never ended with Phil. What had she expected? Him to come back to her once the police was done with him? To confess his love and then live happily ever after with her? Ridiculous! He wasn't the type and neither was she.

"I'm sorry, Sofie." Phil's voice sounded distant and tormented. She had saved his life and he was re-paying her poorly. "I never wanted to put you in danger."

Sofie looked at him. The truth in his statement was obvious. He was a player and schemer but he would never let physical harm come to anyone around him. Neither his clients nor her.

"I know."

Relief flushed his eyes as he sank to his knees next to her chair. "Thank you," he breathed, leaning his forehead against her thigh.

Sofie instinctively reached down to stroke his hair. His thick brown strains ran through her fingers and it felt like they were back in the Meadow. When everything was simple and easy. When all it took was swooping into his life and taking him away from all the lies and madness. Maybe it wasn't too late. Sofie cupped his cheeks and leaned down to kiss him.

"I can't..." He turned away and got up. Hugging his shoulders, he wanted to say something but decided against it. Was he thinking about feeding her another lie?

"Why do you do this?"

"Because that's how I manipulated or paid people in the past." It pained him to confess this. "And I don't want to do this anymore. I want to pay people with money. That's why I want to hire you to investigate the case. Find something on Lee. So I can get my stocks back."

Of course. Money. That's the reason for everything. Did he even care about the consequences to her?

"What if Lee catches me?"

"He won't hurt you. He needs you. You are his only bargaining chip."

"That's not quite true, is it?" Sofie replied. "There is Ashley and Jasmit and god knows how many other women. Lee might have better leverage with one of them."

"Sofie..." For a moment he was speechless. "He has all the leverage already. I don't want to see any of the others get hurt, but... you are different. I'd do anything to keep you safe, Sofie."

The way he stressed 'anything' let goosebumps rise on Sofie's back.

"Because I saved your life?"

"No. I mean... yes that too, but... " he stopped to gather his thoughts. "Sofie, I am not free. As you put it, I'm trapped in a golden cage. I am bought and sold. And it probably will never stop. I'm in too deep. Have too many secrets. Collectively, they'll never let me go. But if I were free..." Sofie felt the gravity of what he was about to say. "I'd come with you in a heartbeat. The others are beautiful, wealthy and powerful, but nothing comes even close to how I feel when I'm with you."

He wanted her. Over all the others. He said it. This time she wasn't imagining it. It was there plain and clear. But could she believe him?

"Philip..." Sofie shook her head, "It's hard to tell what's the truth with you. You are so good at... pretending."

He closed his eyes. If he was telling the truth it would have been a hard blow. Hearing that she didn't believe him. That he had cried wolf one too many times.

"My real name is Phil. Philón Csasz." The way he pronounced his last name sounded like Chase. "My family is from Hungary. But when I was 14 they sent me to a boarding school here in England and from there to Uni. They invested everything they had in my education. I was meant to become a Psychologist. But when the fees increased... I got into this." He looked out the window, following a flock of sparrows on the horizon. "At first, it was easy money to get me through uni. But when Elandra got involved. The pay got larger and the women I was paired with... they weren't just interested in the sex anymore. They genuinely appreciated having someone to talk to." A sad smile whisked over his face. "In a way, I was still helping people. Except the money was more than I would have ever made as a psychologist. It was a no-brainer. At least that's how it felt back then. But after a while, I wished I'd never fallen in with them, until... now." He turned and took Sofie's hand. "Now all of it has been worth it because it has let me to you."

His confession was raw and sudden. It touched her heart in a way that took her breath away.

"I want to be done with the secrets," he continued, "and I wish there was a way out of this mess. But if there isn't... I want to remember us. Imagine what might have been. But for that I need you to believe me."

Sofie felt tears well in her eyes. She'd never felt so conflicted before. His words sounded real. They sure were what she'd been dying to hear. But he didn't act the part. And if there's one thing she knew as a journalist it was that only actions mattered.

"You never kiss me first." She picked the first tangible thing that was a red flag to her. "You always hold back, even when you wore the mask and I didn't know who you were."

"It felt wrong to deceive you like that."

"But it's ok to pretend you were someone else to get me here?"

"My plan was to set up the meeting with Lee and then call you. I didn't expect to run into you at the ball. And when I saw you..."

"...you wanted to play?"

"No!" Hesitantly he added, "I wanted to meet you new. Without any background. Not as Philip. I wanted to see how you would react. If you treated other men differently. I guess I wanted to know whether I was special."

Sofie swallowed. She had treated them exactly the same. She flirted with both. Was stringing them along. Only to then use them for her own gain. Nothing has changed. That's what he'd concluded. He acknowledged his feelings for her, embraced them, while she went straight back to her old tricks.

"How does that prove anything? It was you all along"

There was a rugged edge in her voice. It dawned on her that she indeed had his heart until she'd lost it yesterday.

"But you didn't know that. You didn't recognize me."

"So that's your answer then?"

"Yes." He looked down. "But that's ok! Actually, it's a relief. I have to go back to being Philip. And it's easier if I know that this won't affect you."

"Why wouldn't this affect me?" She refused to accept this conclusion without having her say. She lifted his chin. "Phil, look at me..."

He caught her hands.

"You feel hot!"

"What?"

He touched a hand to her forehead.

"You're burning up. Let's get you to a hospital. We need to know for sure what he injected."

Sofie's head was spinning. Had she been wrong about the injection? Was her body in overdrive to fight an infection? Or was it her head, trying to make sense of Phil's emotional rollercoaster? The only way to know for sure was to find out what Lee had done, for both their sakes. If he injected her with a pathogen, it would be reckless not to get on top before she might be contagious.

"Fine," she conceded, "but no hospital, I have a place to go."

She got up from her chair.

"And Phil... this conversation is not over yet!"

Into the great unknown

Sofie leaned against the door frame. This was the place. It had been a while since she was here last but she remembered it well. The pale-white neon lights flickered against her skin, creating deep shadows under her eyes. And the strange chemical smell made her stomach turn. Or was that because her head was still spinning from her conversation with Phil. They could have had a future together had she not screwed it up. Had she not -- once again -- used him as a stepping stone. Proved that she was incapable of seeing people as more than her informants.

"We should have gone to a hospital."

Phil watched her walk unsteadily into the dimly lit room, holding on to the wall for support. This place wasn't a medical facility. It didn't even have the right implement. It was the cellar of an office block, stuffed with laboratory equipment that looked outdated and barely operational. The style and color of the bench tops was mismatched and the fume hoods had different heights. The whole lab looked salvaged and barely more functional than a scrapyard.

Before Sofie could answer, a plump man with black hair and terracotta skin entered the room. His tattered lab coat hung off one shoulder and he was slightly out of breath. He had been running to get here.

"Sofia! Meu carinho," he shouted with a heavy Brazilian accent. Storming toward Sofie, he planted three wet kisses on her cheeks before surveying her doleful condition. "So, what did you get yourself into this time?"

"Oh you know, this and that."

Staying lighthearted was her defence mechanism. She held up the syringe she snatched while Phil had Lee pinned against the wall.

"I have a sample for you to analyze, Perro."

"Always happy to peel the pineapple for you, Bebê."

Even though Perro had been living in the UK for a decade he still translated Portuguese expressions one to one, creating the oddest phrases.

He put on gloves. The latex slapped against his skin, blowing out a little puff of talcum powder. He took the syringe and held it up against the light.

"Not much left," he commented to no one in particular before pipetting the remaining content into a small plastic vial. When he finished he nodded towards Phil.

"So, who's the observer?"

"I can't tell you. You know that."

"Sure, I'm not looking for horns on the horse's head." Sofie had no idea what that meant but it sounded defensive. "...it's just. I thought this was our thing."

"You aren't jealous Perro, are you?" Sofie forced a laugh. In the past, they barely exchanged three words beyond the excuberat welcome. Especially not about personal things. It had been easy and efficient, and Sofie liked it that way.

Perro took the hint and laughed as if Sofie made a joke rather than a poignant observation. He picked up the sample and returned to work when Phil interjected.

"He's not jealous. He's worried that you won't come back. That he won't be part of your investigations in the future."

"What?"

Sofie was gobsmacked. How did Phil get all that from one question?

"Well," Perro admitted, "I could understand if you wanted to use a better lab. But I thought you came here..." His eyes searched hers. "Because you liked my work."

Sofie gave him a reassuring smile. She breathed out a small sigh, she knew what this was about. Perro wanted to have his ego stroked.

"You are the most brilliant scientist I know. So why would I go to a flashy lab when they probably can't find the answers I need. No Perro, you'll always be my go-to scientist."

Perro's cheeks flushed, giving Phil a smug sideways look. "That means a lot coming from you, Sofia". He cleared his throat. "Ok, let's see what's in the sample."

He pressed a button of one of his machines and a deep rumble started inside the metal casing. As Perro studied the readings on the touch screen, Sofie threw a scolding look at Phil. Why had he been kicking up dust? But the look he gave her back was that of sad confirmation. It said 'You did it again. You used him'.

"Results are ready."

Perro's voice interrupted the accusing silence that was growing between Sofie and Phil like a storm front on an autumn's day. With a final ping the screen changed from showing the run statistics to plotting the result. It was a graph with a black horizontal line and three large spikes.

"That's strange," Perro mumbled. "Only sodium chloride."

"What's that?" Sofie queried.

"The chromatogram, here..." He pointed to the spiky graph. "It only shows sodium chloride as the largest peak. And the other two are just the signature of H2O."

"And in English?"

"It seems your sample only contains salt water."

Sofie let out the breath she didn't realize she was holding. It was a relief to hear it confirmed, even if she was pretty sure she'd guessed right.

"Yes, that's good."

"Oh? You've been expecting that?" Perro sounded disappointed.

"Yes," Sofie laughed. "Not everything can be explosives or poison. I'm sure the next sample I'll bring you will be more exciting again. Thanks for your help Perro, this was really important to me."

A satisfied smile stretched Perro's lips.

"Hang on, what are those squiggly lines?" Phil pointed to a couple smaller peaks at the end of the graph.

"Oh that? It's just noise. Some random atoms the machine picked up."

"Atoms of what? I feel like we are missing something."

"Missing? It's all right here. And I tell you: it's nothing."

"Humor me. What if those peaks were higher. What would they stand for?"

"Silicium and a couple of different metals. Probably minor contamination from the needle."

"I somehow sense this is important." Phil rubbed over the stubbles on his chin. Something was bothering him.

"What are you thinking?" Sofie asked.

"Not sure yet. He was hiding something. Something to do with the sample."

"Your sensing?" Perro mocked. "C'mon, Sofia! Who's the clown? Some sort of psychic?'

"No such things as psychics," Phil replied, ignoring Perro's derogative tone. "I read people."

"Their minds? Or what?"

"If you will. Only 7% of our conversations are words. The rest are small subconscious clues, like the tone of our voice or the gestures we use. I know how to interpret the subcontext. Hear the 93% of what we don't say."

"Oh yes? Then tell me what I'm thinking right now," Perro challenged.

"It's not a party trick."

"Humour me."

"Fine, you are thinking 'if this clown wasn't here I'd ask Sofia out for ice-cream' "

Perro stared at Phil. The embarrassment had turned his ears red and he was chewing his tongue as if to bite back insults.

"Well you are wrong," he finally spat, before turning to Sofie. "I take it you have all you need from me. Because I have things to do."

"Yes, Perro, thank you again for your help." Sofie tried to ignore his humiliation.

"Anytime."

With a last glare towards Phil, Perro walked out, leaving the two alone in his makeshift lab.

"How did you know what he was thinking?"

"He's obviously fascinated by your work and wants to know more. He probably wanted to ask you out for a couple of visits now."

"Ok. But why ice-cream. That's oddly specific."

"He'd never ask you for a dinner date. He's too insecure for that. And coffee is too cliche for a scientist. So, ice cream is suitably casual, yet creative enough for his standards."

"That's a hunch."

"He kept licking his teeth whenever he looked at you. It wasn't anything sexual, he isn't the type to objectify women. And..." Phil grinned, "I saw him walk in with a flyer from a newly opened Gelato place just around the corner."

"You cheated..."

"What? I knew what he wanted to do. Knowing where he'd taken you was just the cherry on top. Literally."

"Fine," Sofie smiled, before becoming more serious. "So, you know how to read people but you can't read me?"

"Who says I can't?"

"You see me as some kind of manipulative monster who cons people into helping."

"Sofie it's alright. I'm not judging you. It's human nature to manipulate when it's for the greater good. I guess that's why it's called a 'white lie'."

"What do you mean?"

"At uni we learned about this one experiment where people had to think of a number between 1 and 6," Phil recalled. "Then they rolled a dice and if the number they thought of matched the eyes on the dice they got 5 Pounds. Guess how often people were right."

"Easy, 1 in 6. If they didn't cheat."

"Exactly. But they observed a success rate of 2 in 6. So a couple of people pretended they thought of the right number to pocket the money. There are always some crooks. Right? But what do you think happened when the money was instead donated to charity?"

"It went down to 1 in 6, I guess. There's no incentive to lie, if they can't keep the money."

"Sounds plausible," Phil nodded, "but instead almost all participants started to cheat. With money going to a good cause, cheating had turned into a 'white lie'."

"What's your point?"

"You manipulate people to get to the truth. And for you that's ok because you make the world a better place. One story at a time."

Sofie took a deep breath, trying not to feel hurt.

"I might persuade my informants to talk. Maybe manipulate them into giving me more than they intended to. But that's not what I'm doing with you. I feel..."

"Stop the games Sofie. I didn't tell you how I felt to get a response or make you feel bad. I just wanted to end the secrets between us before I have to go back to Elandra."

"Ok. Yes, I was playing a game at the beginning, but then..." Sofie suddenly felt self-conscious. "Everything changed. I have feelings for you, Phil. And it scares me. Because when I let my guard down, people die."

He studied her. Hearing what she wasn't saying.

"That's what happened to the last man you loved, isn't it?"

"Yes."

What would Damien say to her right now? Would he blame her? Be angry? Or give her permission to move on? With Phil? When she regained her composure, she asked the question that had been on her mind since Phil gave himself up to Lee.

"Why are you really going back to Elandra?"

"To protect you. It's the only way I know how."

"But I don't need protecting."

Sofie had to smile when she saw Phil's expression. He looked as if she had single handedly killed chivalry.

"I have drug cartels, crime lords and dodgy governments wanting to kill me already. By now, adding a murderous London business man to the list is a drop in the ocean."

He did not reply. Was he offended? Or shocked?

"No more secrets. Right? That goes both ways. As far as I'm concerned you are the one who needs protecting."

"From what?"

"From the people who hunt me, I guess. If you were to come with me. Nothing would ever be predictable again. It's the great unknown." Sofie's eyes sparkled. "You once said that at Elandra you get to talk to 'interesting and accomplished' people. Well, I can give you that and more. With me you'd be free to travel the world. Talking to people who need our help and the ones who need to be brought to justice. You will have to be the smartest person in the room." She lowered her voice. "Because if you're not you'll probably die. It's dangerous. It's underground. And the line between right and wrong sometimes gets blurred. It would be very different to what you are used to. So the question is can you handle that -- just to be with me?"

Phil swallowed.

"No, Sofie, the only question I need an answer for is can you accept my help. You've been working alone. Calling all the shots. Deciding what's right and what's wrong. But if I'd join you we would be a team. Making decisions together. Be equal. Can you handle that?"

His question was going straight to the core. It was open and vulnerable. There was no need for games anymore or layers to hide behind. She had finally met the real Phil. And she liked what she was seeing.

"Yes," she smiled. "Under one condition: you need to learn the rules first before you get any say in our decisions."

"Deal."

He leaned in to kiss her. His breath was warm and minty and Sofie could see her whole future reflected in his eyes.

"Let's go back to that crappy little house of yours and do something where I do know the rules already."

Lake of darkness

P hil and Sofie arrived at the safe-house as the sun was setting. Golden hour dipped the little cabin in a warm glow. It didn't matter that it was barely liveable, it was a place for them to be together. And that's all that mattered for now.

Sofie fought the little rusty door on the dilapidated front porch. "We need to change that damn lock," she muttered impatiently when Phil wrapped his arms around her.

"We have all the time in the world to fix this up as our home," he breathed against the nape of her neck.

Sofie leaned back into him, feeling his chest rise as he brushed her buttocks against his groin.

"On second thoughts, you better get the door open otherwise I'll have you right here." His hands moved over the curves of her hips with a sudden famishing hunger. "I want you so badly. You've been all I could think about the past couple of weeks."

Sofie let out a small giggle that turned into a moan as his warm lips brushed over her skin. With one last shove the door finally gave way and they tumbled into the living room, bumping the table and chairs. This space was way too small.

Phil backed her against the wall and their mouths melted into each other.

"Do you have any candles?" he rasped as their lips finally parted.

"Are you worried about switching on the lights?" They had been careful coming here. Taking the tube and walking the rest of the way. Sofie was certain they had no tail. No one should know they were here.

"No," Phil laughed, "This is our first time together as you and me. And I want it to be special."

"Oh," Sofie blushed. This had not even occurred to her. But she was glad that one of them had a romantic streak. "I see what I can find."

Heading for the small bathroom he added, "I take a quick shower."

When he returned Sofie had placed thick white candles on the fireplace mantle and next to the bed. Their glow gave the rundown bedroom a rustic-chic feel and Sofie was pleased with the transformation. This actually felt cosy.

"You are so beautiful," Phil breathed, standing in the doorframe with his hair still wet from the shower.

He took her into his arms, cautious and longing, like he could not believe that this was actually real. That they were finally together, without games or agendas.

"And you are naked," Sofie grinned, inhaling his clean soapy scent as she unraveled the towel around his hips.

She let her hand run down his taut belly, feeling him grow hard.

"Do we have a condom?"

"You are mine now." Sofie looked into his hazel-brown eyes. The warmth she saw in them was not the reflection of the candles. It came from deep within. It was the radiating comfort of belonging. "We haven't been with anyone else since getting tested at Elandra and I'm on birth control. I want to feel all of you."

A tempting smile played around his lips. She'd pushed open the door to experiencing his full repertoire. Tonight was a small preview of what was to come, what the rest of their lives would be like. And Sofie couldn't wait to get started.

"Lie down," she commanded. Not breaking eye contact she slowly crawled on top and straddled him. His bare member twitched against the thin fabric of her panties. She let her eyes roam over the handsome man below her. All the scheming and decisions had taken her to this point. All the dangers and risks were worth it. He was worth it all.

She unzipped her dress and lifted it over her head. She needed to feel his skin on hers Sensing her urge, he let his hand slide up her flanks, hooking his thumbs underneath the clasp of her bra, and making her breast spring free. He cupped them and sucked a nipple into his mouth. Lust rolled through Sofie's body as he swirled his tongue around her hardening bud.

Gently tucking his hair to stop his sweet assault, she rasped, "Tonight is about you." She pushed him back onto the bed. "I want you to enjoy this without holding back." As she moved down on him, she let her stiff nipples brush over his chest. "Tonight, I want your pleasure to come first."

She licked along his erection and wrapped her lips around the glistening head. It tasted salty and rousing. She could feel his shaft throbbing in her mouth.

"Sofie, this is so good."

A primal groan came from his throat. She could tell how much he enjoyed being the one indulged for a change and she loved the control she had over his arousal. He was getting harder with each pump and his moans vibrated deep within her core.

"I want to be inside you," he forced out between unsteady breaths.

He leaned forward to grab her hips. Effortlessly he lifted her off his body and rolled on top of her. She opened her legs for him. It was the unspoken invitation to finally be one.

Every nerve in Sofie's body exploded, as he eased into her. Without even trying, the techniques he had perfected over his career pushed Sofie over the edge. Her muscles pulsed around him bringing him close to his own ecstasy. With one more hard thrust, he climaxed. Burying his face into her neck he muffled a moan. He continued to move, riding out their orgasms as long as they could last.

This was perfection and Sofie hoped this moment could last forever. Only the two of them, with the world around them disappearing. No responsibilities, no threats, no promises or obligations. Just the warmth of his skin next to hers, listening to their steady heartbeats.

The candles had burned low and the flickering flames shining through the wax groove tinged the room into a mellow glow. This far into the suburbs, everything was quiet. Even the crickets outside had stopped their ambient concert and the wind rustled the bushes around the house. With a sudden jolt Phil sat up.

"What's wrong?"

"Something's changed. The sounds are different..."

He pulled his pants back on and tossed Sofie his shirt.

"Do you have an alarm system here?"

"No." She realized how much she had veered from her usual protocols in her haste to be with Phil.

He went into the dark kitchen and peered out the cracked glass of the front window. The street was deserted, no cars, no people. It was a cul-de-sac leading to a scrapyard, no one would stroll the streets, especially at night.

He shook his head and let out a small laugh. "I'm sorry, Sofie, I'm being paranoid."

Phil crawled back to bed, pulling her onto the mattress with him.

"But I discovered something after all," he added playfully.

"Oh yes, what's that?"

"You look damn hot in my shirt." He let his fingers slip under the loose fabric to stroke her flat tummy and their lips found each other again.

With a sudden screeching crack the front door flew open and two men in black ski masks stormed the bedroom.

"Don't move," one of them shouted, pointing his gun at Sofie.

The bright torch he held underneath his gun blinded her and she lifted her arms to shield her eyes.

"I said, don't move!" the masked man growled, deliberately shining his lights directly into Sofie's face.

The other goon tossed a phone to Phil. "Boss has a message for you."

The mobile was on speaker and Lee's voice filled the room.

"Hello Philén."

"How did you find us?" Phil's voice was filled with contempt. He had been so close to having finally escaped. Being finally free from the shadows of his past.

"You don't need to know." The phone made Lee's chuckle an inhumanly croak. "All you need to know is that I'll be able to find you again. Anywhere. Anytime."

Sofie reached for her arm.

"He injected something to track us." Her eyes met Phil's. "The silicon and metal traces... you were right."

"Clever bird," Lee sounded genuinely surprised. "Then I probably should tell you that there is no way to remove the nano-trackers. I injected thousands of them and by now they have spread through your whole body."

"You bastard!" Phil was shaking as he lifted the phone to shout into it. "Why did you inject her when you wanted me?"

"Those little nanobots are experimental. They still have some nasty side effects that would lower your market value. And I need you to perform as Elandra's Primo." His amusement turned to business. "In fact, I need you to do that tonight. I've set up a rendezvous with Siri Tommer. That's why Yates and his team are here, they will escort you to Elandra now."

Yates! Phil searched the masked faces for hints that would identify the former Elandra guard.

"The information you gave me on Ms. Tommer checked out but I need more. She'll appear at the Royal Commission hearing tomorrow. And I want to know what she's going to say before the press does and the markets move."

"I can't do that."

"What do you mean 'can't'?"

"He's blown his load already, Boss," one of the goons snickered. "Being with his little floosie."

"Don't be ridiculous, Yates." Lee's voice sounded exacerbated, "He is used to that. You know as well as I do that Elandra runs multiple sessions a day." Lee paused to consider his approach. "Yates, I think you need to convince him to perform."

The goon took off his mask. After having been outed by Lee, there was no need for secrecy anymore. His sturdy built, pale green eyes and hairstyle made him look like an average football hooligan.

"How convincing am I allowed to be, Boss?"

"Do what you must." Lee sighed. "But only to the girl. Philón needs to stay presentable."

Yates licked his lips. "Roger that, Boss."

The phone line disconnected. Lee was not going to listen in on the maiming and torturing Yates asked permission for. He just wanted to have the results, he did not care how they were achieved.

"Yates," Phil stepped forward, "let's make a deal here..."

"I had enough of your deals. The last one put me straight into the nuthouse. I'd still be there if Lee didn't pull me out." He flashed his teeth and moved closer to Sofie. "Refuse to come with us one more time, Pillip, and I'll have some fun with her. I'll make you watch how I'm..."

"He is not going anywhere with you," Sofie lifted her chin and glared at the hooligan.

Looking at Phil, she lightly nodded her head towards the fireplace mantel and the bedside table. She only hoped that Phil understood her reckless plan.

"Go," she shouted and they both grabbed a candle and splashed the molten wax into the goons' faces. Before Yates could recover from the boiling viscose liquid running over his eyes and mouth, Sofie grabbed his gun and fired two rounds into his chest, like she had trained hundreds of times before.

Phil's goon was still wearing his ski mask, which protected him from most of the assault. He ripped his mask off and stumbled backwards before Phil could get hold of his gun. Instinctively the thug veered to the side and pointed his gun at Sofie, who had taken aim at him and was about to fire.

"Stop, I'll come with you." Phil lunged between the two guns facing off. "No one else has to die here tonight."

"Oh yes? Says who?" the goon laughed.

He sidestepped Phil and fired at Sofie. With reflexes kicking in, Phil threw himself in front of the shot. He yelped in pain as the bullet tore through his flesh.

A second shot was fired. It lit the room in an eerie yellow flash and created a sickening crack as metal tore through bone. The goon sank to the floor with blood pouring out of a hole between his eyes.

In shock and disbelief Sofie crouched next to Phil. His blood pooled on the floor boards. Sofie could smell the warm metal scent of his lifeblood running out. It created a shimmering lake of darkness in the dimly lit room. In it, Sofie could make out her own reflection. It was a mask of panic and terror.

"Don't leave me," she whispered, unsure whether Phil could still hear her.